"Why

Colin kneaded the tensed muscles bunched around her neck. "You will when you can handle it."

"I can now."

"You're already remembering bits and pieces. It'll fall into place."

The feel of his gentle hands massaging her tension tempted Emma to lean back against him and draw comfort from his embrace. He had given her so much, and she knew his reason was tied up in guilt. "I don't blame you for what happened on the highway. You saved my life."

"I don't think I'll ever forget the accident. I thought I killed you."

Emma twisted around. "You listen to me. I was shot first. If you hadn't been there, they would have finished me off. I owe you my life. And I just realized I haven't thanked you, Colin Fitzpatrick. You're a good man."

Books by Margaret Daley

Love Inspired Suspense

Hearts on the Line #23
Heart of the Amazon #37
So Dark the Night #43

Love Inspired

The Power of Love #168
Family for Keeps #183
Sadie's Hero #191
The Courage to Dream #205
What the Heart Knows #236
A Family for Tory #245
*Gold in the Fire #273
*A Mother for Cindy #283

*Light in the Storm #297
The Cinderella Plan #320
*When Dreams Come True #339
*Tidings of Joy #369

*The Ladies of Sweetwater Lake

MARGARET DALEY

feels she has been blessed. She has been married for more than thirty years to her husband, Mike, whom she met in college. He is a terrific support and her best friend. They have one son, Shaun. Margaret has been writing for many years and loves to tell a story. When she was a little girl, she would play with her dolls and make up stories about their lives. Now she writes these stories down. She especially enjoys weaving stories about families and how faith in God can sustain a person when things get tough. When she isn't writing, she is fortunate to be a teacher for students with special needs. Margaret has taught for over twenty years and loves working with her students. She has also been a Special Olympics coach and has participated in many sports with her students.

So Dark the Night

MARGARET DALEY

Steeple
Hill®

Published by Steeple Hill Books™

STEEPLE HILL BOOKS

Steeple
Hill®

ISBN-13: 978-0-373-44233-5
ISBN-10: 0-373-44233-1

SO DARK THE NIGHT

www.SteepleHill.com

Printed in U.S.A.

The God of my strength, in whom I will trust;
My shield and the horn of my salvation,
My stronghold and my refuge;
My Savior, You saved me from violence.
—*2 Samuel* 22:3

To the students I've taught—you are the best!

ONE

Emma St. James drove down the lane that led to her brother's cabin on an Illinois lake. The overhanging oak and maple trees shaded the road, heightening the darkness beginning to creep over the landscape with the approach of dusk. When she pulled up to the side of the large log cabin, she parked in the back next to Derek's black Ford truck and rested her forehead on the steering wheel for a moment. Exhaustion clung to her like a second skin.

The past few weeks had been frantic, nonstop work, one photo shoot after another, that had left her little time even to sleep. She'd been thankful when her older brother had insisted she spend a few days with him during a brief pause in her work schedule. Derek could always make her feel better, even if his invitation had seemed strange to her. He needed to talk to her about something important and hadn't wanted to do it over the phone.

Climbing from her yellow Thunderbird convertible, Emma stretched her aching muscles and rolled her head in a slow circle. The long drive from New York had finally caught up with her, and all she wanted to do was take a hot shower and go to bed. She didn't think she could put two coherent sentences together. She and her brother would have to catch up in the morning.

She reached behind the driver's seat and plucked her red leather purse from the back, then headed for the front porch. That was when she spied the white Firebird on the other side of the cabin, partially hidden behind some large honeysuckle bushes, their scent perfuming the cooling spring air. Strains of classical music wafted from the cabin. Company? That was the last thing she wanted at the moment. She moved toward the window near the door to see who was visiting her brother. After the past week of avoiding the press who wanted to verify yet another false story about her, she wanted to make sure it wasn't a reporter who had somehow found out where she would be for the next few days.

Peering into the cabin, she noticed two men, one vaguely familiar, hovering over her brother, who sat in a straight-backed lattice chair, his wide eyes fixed on the taller of the pair.

I've seen that man somewhere. But where?

With fear stamped on his features, Derek was talking and shaking his head. That was when she noticed her brother's hands were tied behind his back. Emma opened her purse and stuck her hand inside, fumbling in the depths. Lipstick. Compact. Wallet. She looked down. Where was her cell phone? A slapping sound brought her attention back to the men in the cabin. The tall, thin man struck her brother across the mouth a second time, his head jerking back. Blood gushed from between his lips and rolled down his chin. Emma gasped, starting for the door.

Out of the corner of her eye, she caught the flash of

metal in the short, bulky man's hand as he came forward. Paralyzed, she stopped.

What in the world was going on? Was that a gun?

Again she delved into her oversized purse, trying to find her cell phone. She needed help and hoped she could get some before—

The sound of a gunshot rocketed through her. As if hit, she staggered back, dropping her bag.

Through the window she saw her brother slump over. A scream welled up inside her. Her hand over her mouth, she backed away, desperate to keep the scream inside.

No!

She blinked as though that would erase the horror she saw through the window. Taking another step back, her gaze glued to the scene inside the cabin, she bit down on her hand. The ropes about her brother's chest held him up, but the bright red of his blood filled her vision. Tears sprang to her eyes. She had to get help.

Please let Derek still be alive.

She spun around to flee and bumped into a bench, sending it flying off the porch. The crashing sound reverberated through her mind. She glanced over her shoulder. The tall man looked up, his cold, dark eyes fixed on her. She shuddered.

Run! her mind shouted.

She leaped off the porch and started for her car. Halfway there she realized she had no keys. They were in her purse on the porch! Frantic, she slowed a few paces, scanning the terrain.

No time to get the keys. Where could she hide? The woods? The shed? Behind the cabin?

The banging of the door against the logs of the wall

sent her racing toward the woods. The report of a gun pierced the air at the same time a bullet hit a tree trunk a few feet to her left, pieces of bark flying outward. With pounding feet that matched the racing of her heart, she tore into the forest, praying the dark shadows enveloped her and hid her from their view. Gasping for air, she kept running, afraid to stop and find a place to hide for fear they would find her.

Branches ripped at her face and body. She stumbled and fell to her knees. Pain shot up her legs. Pushing herself to her feet, she clawed her way up a small ridge, littered with underbrush and stubby trees. One of her sandals caught on a limb. She tugged, the shoe coming off and tumbling down the incline. Emma stared at the bright red leather that reminded her so much of the blood she'd seen on Derek. She shoved that image away. She couldn't think about that now. She had to get him help. *She had to stay alive.*

She started back down the ridge. In the distance she heard the two men tearing through the woods. Not far away. No time to get her shoe. Spinning back around, she looked about her to see which way she should go. Deeper into the woods? Or toward the highway?

The crashing sound of the men tracking her, who obviously didn't care if she heard them, dominated her thoughts as she tried to decide. The closer the sound came, the more frenzied her heart beat. Panting, she headed for the darkness of the denser trees on the other side of the ridge, away from the highway.

Deeper and deeper she pushed into the forest. Something sharp cut the bottom of her bare foot. She didn't stop to see what it was. She kept going, an ache in her side intensifying and rivaling the pain from the wound on her heel.

The farther she went, the darker it became until she could barely make out the area ten feet in front of her. Her lungs burned. Her eyes stung from the tears that loomed just beneath the surface. Holding her side, she stopped by a large trunk, leaning into it for support as she drew in large gulps of air. Her legs quivering, she listened.

For a few seconds silence tantalized her with visions of a successful escape. Then the sound of breaking twigs and a muffled voice resonated through the trees. They had followed her into the woods. They weren't far behind.

Scanning the black curtain around her, she glimpsed the faint outline of some large bushes. She dove toward them, seeking their shelter. Darkness and leaves cocooned her in safety. The scent of earth and vegetation peppered the air. She waited.

An eternity later, she heard plodding footsteps approaching. Every muscle tensed to the point of pain. She waited, not even daring to breathe much.

"Ouch! Watch it, will you?"

The rough voice pierced the quiet and sent Emma's heart racing even more. Not far away. She squinted and peered out into the gloom. Nothing but faint shapes of trees surrounded by blackness.

"We ain't gonna find her. Let's get back and check her out. Probably Derek's latest girlfriend. Fancy car means she has to have money."

"Will you shut up? I can't hear a thing over your constant chattering."

The man who belonged to the rough voice must be the leader, Emma thought and decided it was the tall man she'd seen at the cabin, the one with the cold, black eyes. She'd never forget those eyes as he'd stared at her through the window, Derek's limp form next to him. Again she pictured the man with the chilling eyes. The niggling sensation she'd seen him before wouldn't loosen its grip on her thoughts.

Where have I seen him? Who is he? Why did they shoot my brother?

Oh, Derek. Tears crowded her throat. What if her brother was still alive? She needed to get him help, and time was against her.

"What's the point? It's too dark anyway," the other one said, his voice higher. It riveted Emma back to the problem at hand.

If she was right, that was the man who'd shot her brother. Throat tightening, she squeezed her eyes closed, trying to keep the tears inside. She didn't have time to think beyond getting to safety. She'd fall apart later.

"We need some flashlights. I have one in the car and I bet there's one at the cabin."

The voices were nearby. Emma shrank back deeper into the underbrush. Her heartbeat roared in her ears so loud she couldn't make out what the short, bulky man replied.

She tried to run through a relaxation technique she used when stressed, but nothing took the edge off. Even taking deeper breaths didn't calm the loud thumping of her heart. She clamped her hands over her ears, her eyes scrunched closed. Like a child playing peekaboo, she hoped since she couldn't see them, *they* couldn't see *her*.

Minutes ticked away. She waited. Slowly, she opened her eyes and dropped her hands to the damp ground.

Nothing…but the wind rustling the leaves on the bush, a curtain of black shrouding her.

She crawled forward from the depths of the thick underbrush and scanned the darkness. Still, silence greeted her. No sound other than nature's. A bird chirped. A frog croaked. Crickets trilled. The normal sounds of a forest.

She inched farther out of her shelter. She needed to get to the highway for help. Thankfully, she knew the woods surrounding the family cabin and realized if she circled around to the right she could reach the highway, flag down a car and escape the two men—and maybe, just maybe, help her brother.

With her eyes adjusted to the dark, she picked her way through the maze of trees toward what she believed would be the highway. The continual hammering of her heart and the shallow gulps of air made each step difficult. The trembling in her legs spread upward to encompass her whole body. Her pace slowed, shock slipping through her defenses.

Again a sharp object pierced the bottom of her foot. It was too dark even to see where she was stepping. *Can't stop.* She focused all her concentration on lifting one foot and placing it in front of her. Not far, she was sure. She was now glad of all those times she and—a lump lodged in her throat when she thought of her brother. She and Derek had loved to play hide-and-seek in these very woods as children.

The memory produced a tear. It leaked out of her tight restraints and rolled down her cheek. She brushed it away. *No time. Later. Have to keep going. Get help.*

In the distance she heard a car zoom by. She wanted to quicken her pace, but her legs felt as though she wore cement blocks for shoes. Through the trees she saw headlights arc across the terrain and disappear. A hundred feet. Safety. The highway was the only way into town. Her best chance to escape.

Then behind her she heard the two men and saw the beams from their flashlights circling the area in front of them. Her gaze was drawn toward their lights. She was amazed at how fast they had returned. She plowed ahead, forcing herself to go faster. Blocking from her mind the searing pain in her legs and lungs, she limped toward the sounds of passing cars. Fifty feet.

The ribbon of asphalt cut through the forest. Slicing lights illuminated the trees on the edge of the highway. She pushed herself harder. Thirty feet.

The noises behind her grew louder. A light touched the area to the side of her. Then it swept over her as though icy fingers scraped across her. A shout slashed through her thundering heartbeat and sent terror straight to her core.

"There! She's almost to the highway."

"Get her," the rough voice commanded off to the right.

Suddenly Emma didn't see any more headlights on the highway. Darkness surrounded her. Then the beam behind her found her again. She darted to the left, trying to evade the brightness. Ten feet.

In the distance the sound of a car filled the night with hope. She plunged from the cover of the trees and headed toward the headlights barreling down upon her.

A shot rang out from the forest. Panicked, she raced forward.

"Come on, Reverend Fitzpatrick. We're gonna be late. Five miles over the speed limit isn't *really* breaking the law," Brent Hardwood said over the loud music playing on the radio.

Colin Fitzpatrick threw his passenger in the front seat a grin. "Is that your reasoning? No wonder the sheriff has given you several tickets in the past few months."

"Yeah, Brent. One more and your license will be suspended."

Brent twisted around in the seat. "You're no better, Jamie. *You* just haven't been caught. It wasn't that long ago you were drag racing on Miller Road."

"Guys, I don't think I want to hear this. I might be obliged to inform a few parents. And since Neil's dad is the sheriff, it might prove to be a bit awkward."

"Isn't this covered under some confessional rule?" Neil Logan asked from the back seat.

Colin laughed. "No, afraid not."

"Well, it should be," Brent mumbled, his arms folded across his chest. He leaned forward and turned up the radio even more. "This is one of my favorite songs." He began tapping the dashboard to the beat of the music.

Colin settled back, listening to the ribbing among the three teenage boys, each trying to talk over the radio. Best friends. Members of his church. Leaders of the youth group. Today's conference at Central City had been a success. He was already anticipating the young men working with the rest of the youth group to teach them the conflict resolution techniques they had learned.

Maybe he could use the techniques on some of the conflicts he'd found himself caught up in lately. What he really needed was some evasive tactics or disappearing ones. He thought of Mrs. Reed's little matchmaking maneuver last weekend with her niece who had come to visit for the month. He'd barely escaped that trap. He'd been married once to a wonderful woman. He didn't see himself marrying again.

"Reverend, my big sis wants you to come in after you drop me off."

Brent's statement caught Colin's full attention for a few seconds. He glanced at the seventeen-year-old and said, "It's been a long day and tomorrow is a school day."

"Mary will be mighty disappointed. I think she baked you a German chocolate cake. She promised me a slice if I could get you to come in."

"While I appreciate—"

Something darted out of the trees and plunged toward his car. Colin slammed his foot on the brake at the same time the person—a woman—halted in the middle of the road, her shocked expression reflected in the glare of his headlights.

Emma stopped on the pavement, the car careening toward her. Paralyzed for a few precious seconds, she stared at the set of bright lights coming at her. *Move!* her mind screamed. *Now!*

Life flooded back into her legs, and she began to lunge toward the opposite side of the road—away from the killers. Pain exploded in her left shoulder, spinning her back into the path of the car.

Colin swerved the wheel of his SUV hard, trying to avoid the woman. Just as he thought he would, she twisted back toward his car. Even though his vehicle was slowing down, he couldn't stop fast enough. The shouts from his passengers and the loud music drowned out the sound of him striking the person, but he felt the impact as though it vibrated through him to his soul. She reeled off the front end of his bumper while he fought to control his SUV. Fishtailing a few feet farther, his car finally came to a stop.

"Is everyone all right?" Colin checked his passengers, his hands shaking so much they slipped from the wheel.

"Yeah," Brent answered, straining to see out the window.

"Man! What was that? A deer?" Jamie Zamets asked, his eyes wide as he craned his neck around to see behind them.

"Do you think it's dead?" Neil asked from the back seat, the shaken tone to his question making it come out as a whisper.

"It was a woman," Brent said, unbuckling his seat beat.

"Stay put." Colin forced all the command he had learned in the army into his voice. He was afraid of what he would find when he got out and he didn't want the teenagers to see.

Colin hurried from the vehicle, slamming the door to emphasize the fact that he wanted the boys to stay in the car. He ran around the back of his vehicle and came to a skidding stop six feet from the rear bumper.

Lying on the pavement was a slim, petite figure, dressed in pants and a shirt, the darkness obscuring the woman's features, the illumination from the taillights not strong enough for him to assess her injuries. Colin knelt to feel for a pulse. A faint beat beneath his fingertips sent relief through him. The scent of blood assailed his nostrils. She was alive but for how long?

"Rev, I thought you might need—" Brent's sentence

came to an abrupt halt as the flashlight he carried caught the victim in its glare.

"She's beautiful," the teen finally murmured.

Colin's gaze skimmed over the woman's face, bleeding from scratches that had nothing to do with the wreck. Beneath the cuts, he had to acknowledge, were very pleasing features, framed by a mass of long black curls. "Here, let me have that and you get back in the car."

The slamming sound of two doors slashed through the silence. Colin knew there was no way he would be able to protect them now.

"Is she dead?" Jamie asked, coming up beside Brent.

"No. Don't you all know how to follow directions?"

"Thought you might want my cell phone, Reverend."

Colin heard Neil's words, but he felt as if he was back in the army, bending over a wounded comrade, because what riveted his attention now was the gaping hole in the young woman's shoulder, blood oozing out of it and pooling on the pavement. His head came up. He scanned the terrain alongside the highway, trying to peer into the dense woods, but he couldn't see anyone, only dark shadows cast by the tall pines and oaks.

From the way she had spun, the shot had to have come from the right side of the road, probably from that thick line of trees, not far from his car. Too close. Hairs on the nape of his neck tingled. Danger resounded in his mind.

"Get back into the car," he said in the toughest voice he could muster.

"But—" Brent started to protest.

"Go. I'll take care of her. Call for help, Neil."

At that moment a pair of headlights crested the hill

and came toward them, followed by another set. Colin shifted his body to shield the woman as the boys trudged back to the car, muttering their disappointment. The tension in his body relaxed a little when he heard the doors slamming on his SUV.

Dear Lord, please protect us from whoever shot this woman. Let this be help arriving. Keep her and the boys safe.

He used his flashlight to flag down the approaching vehicle, hoping there would be safety in numbers, all the while keeping his body between the line of trees and the woman lying on the pavement.

"I might be able to hit her, Roy," the stocky man whispered from the dark cover of the woods.

Hunkered down next to him, Roy took in the scene as more and more people stopped to help the man in the car. "Too risky. If she makes it, we'll take care of her later. Come on. Let's get out of here." He tugged on Manny's gun arm.

"I know I can."

"Listen, you have what, a few bullets left? There's a time to take a stand. And a time to retreat."

"But she saw us."

Roy noticed the large man who'd hit the woman raise his head and look toward where they were hidden. Somehow he got the distinct impression the man had heard them even though they were seventy feet away and talking so low it would take someone with super abilities to hear them. For a few seconds he felt as though it were noon and they were exposed for all to see—at least, for the man who drove the SUV.

A third car stopped at the scene of the wreck. Too many people. Whenever he got an itch that needed scratching, Roy knew it was time to cut his losses. He slipped back into the denser underbrush, keeping his eyes trained on the large man hovering over the woman. There was something menacing about him, Roy thought, remembering when the man discovered the woman had been shot. Alertness had stiffened him, his sharp gaze taking in his surroundings as if guns and shootings were an everyday occurrence for him.

A few yards into the woods Roy pivoted and headed back toward the cabin, pleased to hear his partner following. Their employer wouldn't be too happy to hear about this, especially when they hadn't been able to discover the packet they'd been sent to retrieve. Manny might think the woman posed a problem for them, but Roy knew otherwise. Their employer didn't take too kindly to people who messed up.

The woman's eyes snapped open and looked right at Colin. The honey-brown of her gaze pinned him. He leaned forward to listen to her whispered words.

"Help…Derek."

"Where is he?"

She blinked. Terror and pain twisted her features. "I can't…" She licked her lips. "I can't…see." She tried to move, winced and groaned. Her eyelids slid closed. "Derek. Help…him."

"Where is he?" Colin turned so his ear was only inches from her mouth.

"Plea…" Her voice faded, only a faint wisp of breath touching his ear.

Colin straightened, scanning the faces of the people standing nearby in a semicircle. "Is anyone a doctor?"

A woman, who had just arrived, stepped forward. "I'm a nurse. Let me see what I can do."

The middle-aged nurse assessed the damage while removing her sweater and pressing it into the woman's shoulder to stop the flow of blood. "Has anyone called 9-1-1?"

"Yes."

"This woman was shot. What happened?" The nurse looked up at Colin.

He shook his head. "I don't know."

The sound of sirens mingled with the whispers of the people gathered. Another car stopped and two men got out, hanging back from the crowd around the woman.

"Is either one of you a doctor?" Colin asked the new arrivals, hearing the desperate edge to his words. This woman couldn't die. *Please, God, keep her alive. I've seen enough people dying to fill five lifetimes.* Memories threatened to swamp him with emotions he never wanted to relive.

The taller of the two said, "No, sorry."

Colin returned his attention to the woman on the pavement, her petite frame silhouetted by the headlights from several cars. Her dark pants were torn in places as well as her short-sleeved shirt.

She wore only one sandal. He glanced around for her lost shoe. He didn't see it. He examined the bottom of her bare foot. Cuts and dirt greeted his inspection as though she had been running through the woods without one shoe for a long distance. Red-painted toenails taunted him with the mystery that surrounded this woman.

Who was Derek?

Who had shot her?

Where had she come from?

The shriek of the sirens came to a stop as the ambulance pulled up. Colin moved back to allow the paramedics to examine the woman. A sheriff's deputy, a member of his congregation, climbed from his cruiser and walked toward him.

"Can you tell me what happened here, Reverend?"

The three teenagers clambered out of the SUV and hurried toward the deputy, all talking at once.

Colin waved at them to be silent. "John, I was driving home from the youth conference when this woman ran out in front of my car. I thought I was going to be able to avoid her until she spun around and lunged into my path."

Brent nodded. "She came right at us. Someone shot her!"

"Shot? Then this isn't a car accident?" the deputy asked.

"No," all the teenagers answered.

"Excuse me. I need to call this in. Get more help out here."

While the deputy walked to his cruiser, Colin's focus shifted to the woman being wheeled to the ambulance. He wished he could follow the ambulance to the hospital. If he hadn't been on the highway, would she have made it safely to the other side? That was a question he was afraid would plague him for a long time. She had been shot, but how extensive were the injuries caused by his SUV? He couldn't stop the questions from coming. Who was she? Who was Derek? Who shot her? Why?

When the deputy came back, he said, "You all will have to go down to the station to make a statement."

"Even them?" Colin hated the boys being involved.

"I'm afraid so. Neil's dad will be out here shortly. He'll take you in and get your statements."

Brent, Jamie and Neil looked at one another, their eyes wide.

"Can we call our parents to tell them we'll be late getting home?" Jamie held up his cell phone.

"Sure." John Edwards pulled Colin over to the side away from the three teenagers. "Did you see anyone chasing her?"

"No, everything happened so fast." In his mind Colin could see her frozen in his headlights for a few seconds before she started moving again. Then the awful moment when she spun back toward him, her eyes wide with terror. "John, there may be someone else in trouble. Someone named Derek. Before she passed out, she said something about Derek needing help. At least, I think that was it."

"Derek St. James? He has a cabin not too far from here. I hadn't heard he was back in town, though."

"Maybe that's who she was talking about." Colin shook his head. "I don't know."

"I'll check it out after this scene is secured."

"Be careful. Someone in the woods has a gun." Colin realized he was stating the obvious, but he couldn't shake the feeling someone was watching him. Chills encased him in a cold sweat. He threw a last glance toward the area where he thought someone had hidden and shot at the mystery woman. "Look over that way. I think that was where the shot came from."

"I thought you didn't see anything?"

"Nothing like a person or a flash when the gun went

off. I didn't even hear anything with the music on in the car and the windows up. I was too busy trying to avoid the woman. But from the way she spun and fell, that has to be the place. Good cover for a shooter." He knew more than he wished about guns, cover and death.

"I'll have the crime-scene boys check it out."

Heading toward the teenagers, Colin took a calming breath, a coldness embedded deep in his bones. Crystal Springs might be near Chicago, but crime rarely occurred in his little corner of the world, one of the reasons he had been so attracted to the town. It had always been a safe place to raise a family. But the shooting of this woman had altered all that. Deep in his gut he felt their peaceful little slice of heaven was about to change. Icy tentacles burrowed deeper. He shook, his hands balled at his side so tightly that pain zipped up his arms.

TWO

Colin paced from one end of the waiting room to the other. The strong antiseptic odor reminded him of what he disliked most about his job—visiting people in the hospital. His wife had died at Bayview County Hospital, and every time he stepped into its corridors, he remembered Mary Ann's lingering death from cancer. The clean, disinfectant smells, sounds of beeping machines and murmured voices made his stomach clench whenever he came here. He needed to get past his automatic reaction. But even after four years, he hadn't been able to.

"Reverend, she's been moved from recovery to her room now," a nurse at the door said.

Colin nodded, forcing his stomach muscles to relax. Drawing in a deep, fortifying breath, he headed for Emma St. James's private hospital room. Dread leadened his steps. He hadn't seen her since the ambulance had taken her away from the wreck. First, he had been at the sheriff's headquarters giving a statement about the accident, then when he had finally arrived at the hospital two hours ago, Emma St. James had already been wheeled into surgery to have her shoulder repaired.

A deputy stood at her door. "Good afternoon, Reverend."

"Hi, Kirk. How's your wife doing?"

"Better. She should be at church this Sunday."

Colin started to enter the hospital room, but Kirk held up his hand. "Sorry, the sheriff is inside questioning the woman."

Colin leaned against the wall and crossed his arms over his chest. The sights and sounds he had come to know so well when Mary Ann had been here surrounded him. Slowly, any relaxation he had achieved dissolved, leaving him tense again. Time crawled by painfully slowly. A doctor was paged. A phone rang at the nurses' station. An orderly wheeled a patient to the elevator.

The door to Emma's room swung open, and J. T. Logan left, followed by a tall, slender woman with short brown hair. Colin pushed himself away from the wall, preparing to go into the room.

"Reverend, I hope you can help her." J.T.'s deep, gruff voice halted Colin's progress.

"You told her about her brother?"

J.T. gave a curt nod. He gestured toward the woman at his side. "This is Madison Spencer. She's a detective with the state police. She'll be assisting me with the investigation. This is Reverend Fitzpatrick."

"The man who hit her?" Madison angled her head toward the sheriff. "Are you so sure him visiting is a good idea?"

Colin flinched at the bald truth. How was he going to help Emma St. James when his SUV had struck her and he was riddled with guilt?

"If anyone can help her, it'll be Colin."

The sheriff's words fueled Colin's self-confidence until he saw the woman's pinched frown and her assessing expression. "Could she give you any information?"

"No. She doesn't remember much and—" J.T. glanced toward the closed door "—she can't—" his dark gaze fixed on Colin "—see."

"She's blind?"

"Yes."

"Because of the accident?" Colin's heartbeat accelerated, his throat dry.

"I haven't had a chance to talk with the doctor yet." J.T. started down the hallway. "If she remembers anything, let me know."

Colin stared at the door, a dull gray color. What had he done? *Lord, give me the strength to help this woman.*

"You can go in now, Reverend." Kirk's voice cut into Colin's prayer.

He pushed open the door and entered the room. Bright sunlight streamed through the window and a large bouquet of yellow roses, an elaborate arrangement of lilies and a potted ivy plant already graced the window ledge. Colin looked at the small woman in the bed, her eyes closed, the white sheet and a blanket pulled up over her chest as though she was cold. Her arm with the IV in it lay on top of the blue cover across her midsection.

Slowly she opened her eyes. "Who's there?" she whispered, a raw edge to her voice as though she wasn't used to talking.

Did I do this to her? The question kept playing over and over in Colin's mind as he stood frozen a few feet from the bed. She looked so vulnerable with her face bruised and scratched, a bandaged shoulder peeking out from the top of the covers.

"Who's there?" Panic laced her words. She fumbled for the call button.

Colin stiffened, aware he had caused her undue tension. "I'm Reverend Colin Fitzpatrick."

Her hand relaxing her search, she turned her head toward him, her brow creasing. "I didn't ask for a clergyman to visit."

The defensiveness in her statement firmed his resolve. He would be here for her even if she didn't think she needed his help. That was the least he could do. "I know." He moved closer. "I thought you might like to talk to someone about your brother."

She shrank away from him, her hand clutching the blanket. Her eyes slid closed for a few seconds. "How do I know you're a reverend? For all I know, you could be a member of the press. I'm sure they're having a field day over this."

"If you want, I can get the nurse on duty to vouch for me."

"Don't bother. I don't have anything to talk about."

But her expression told Colin otherwise. The sheen to her brown eyes and the trembling of her hand as she ran it over the blanket indicated her distress more than her words. She bit her teeth into her lower lip and looked away.

Colin pulled a straight-backed chair close to the bed and sat, wanting to tell her how he came to be in her room.

"You're wasting your time, Reverend. I'm beyond saving."

"Why do you say that?"

"Don't you know who I am?"

"Emma St. James."

"The daughter of Marlena Howard. For as long as I can remember my mother has been the screen goddess of America. I can't say that my life has been church bazaars and Sunday school classes."

"So I shouldn't waste my time talking to you?"

"I don't think God even knows I exist." Her hands knotted the blanket.

"Why do you say that?"

"That man who left told me my—" she swallowed hard "—my brother was murdered. He thinks I know something about it. I don't remember anything after pulling up to the cabin. I can't even help—" She squeezed her eyes closed. A tear leaked out the corner and rolled down her cheek. Then another.

The sight of the wet trail robbed him of words. He pushed down his own rising emotions and tried to think of something appropriate to say, some way to offer comfort. But what played across his mind was this woman, paralyzed in the middle of the highway, watching his car coming at her.

"Please leave," she whispered, swiping at her tears.

"Sometimes it's good to talk to someone when you're troubled."

Her lower lip quivered. "I wouldn't know where to begin."

The vulnerability in her voice tore at his heart. "How about the beginning?"

Another tear coursed down her face. "Too long a story. Not enough time."

"I'm a good listener. And I have the time."

She shook her head slightly, then winced as though the movement had caused pain. "I want to be left alone." She settled back on the pillow and closed her eyes.

He rose, hovering over her, a part of him hoping she would change her mind and use him as a sounding board. But the other part needed to leave. The space in the room seemed to shrink to the size of a coffin. His breathing became shallow gasps. The last time he had been responsible for someone being hurt was during the Gulf War. After piecing his life back together, he'd promised himself he would never harm another human being. And he hadn't. Until now. He pivoted toward the door.

He pulled himself together enough to present a calm facade to the people in the hallway, but guilt plagued him all the way to the chapel. Inside the small, dimly lit room, a peace washed over him as he sat in the pew before the altar, clasped his hands together and prayed.

She stumbled, her knees hitting the hard-packed earth first. Pain blasted through her as though a gun had gone off inside her. Hands braced in front of her, she scrambled to her feet and kept moving forward. Every part of her hurt, from the frantic beating of her heart to the soles of her bare feet. But she couldn't stop. The sounds of her pursuers grew closer and closer until she felt talons grip her and swing her around. Two hideous faces loomed in front of her.

Emma bolted up in bed, the sudden motion causing pain. Black. An inky curtain taunted her as she scanned her surroundings. *Where am I? Why do I hurt so much? Why can't I see?*

Then the memories flooded her. The accident. Her brother. The police visiting. The continuous blackness.

She sagged back against the firm mattress, the darkness still there even though her eyes were wide-open. From all the sounds outside her door, it had to be daytime.

Every inch of her hurt. The pounding in her head overshadowed the deep ache in her shoulder, the throbbing in her foot. She touched the bandage, remembering the searing pain that had ripped through her just seconds before… Before what? She couldn't remember. Everything after she had climbed from her T-bird at the cabin was a blank except the pain piercing through her shoulder like a red-hot poker.

The swishing sound of the door opening alerted her to someone entering her room. She automatically looked toward where she believed the door was even though her world was dark, no face materializing before her.

"Who is it?" She hated the need to ask, but she hated even more knowing someone else was in the room seeing her like this. She felt so vulnerable, so alone.

"Your dad, Emma."

The deep baritone of her father's voice sliced through her fragile control, causing every muscle to tense, a different kind of hurt, buried for years, surfacing. She tried to visualize on the black screen in her mind what her father looked like. All she could recall was the last picture she'd seen of him in the newspaper a year before. Grainy, his features vague. The photo of him was at a distance. Like their relationship.

"I've come to take you home."

Her hands curled around the covers. "Where's that? Your home? Mine? Mother's?"

"Mine."

He said it with such force and confidence that Emma blinked. "No."

"What do you mean, no? Your life may be in danger. You're—" He paused as though he couldn't think of a word to describe the condition her life was in. "You're injured. I won't accept your answer."

His powerful voice bombarded her at close range. If she reached out, she could probably touch him. She balled her hands into tighter fists even though the action caused her more pain. She concentrated on the pain streaking up her arm to take her mind off her reeling emotions. "You have no choice. I am not leaving with you."

"You need special care. You need to be protected."

Where were you when I was growing up? She wanted to shout the question at him. Instead, she pressed her lips together to keep from saying anything because she knew it was useless to argue with the man. He was a force to be reckoned with, and right now she had no strength to fight anyone.

"You aren't thinking clearly, Emma. Someone murdered Derek. Someone shot you."

That much she knew. It was all the space between those two events that was blank—like her view of the world through her eyes. Dark. Nothing.

He touched her arm. She winced and tried to pull away, but his fingers clasped around her. She thought of her dream, of the talons gripping her.

Frustration, mixed with hopelessness, swamped her. Tears welled up, but she choked them back. Not in front of this man who didn't have a heart. Never again. Those years long ago crying herself to sleep had taught her the uselessness of tears.

He removed his hand from her arm. "That woman has filled your mind with lies for years."

"It wasn't your choice to divide the family down the middle?"

"The past has nothing to do with the here and now. I have hired a bodyguard for you."

"No. I don't want anything from you. Don't you get it? I can't see. I don't even remember what happened. I'm certainly no help to the sheriff. I'm not a threat to anyone." She searched the covers for the call button. She couldn't take another moment with the man who had given her up and never had anything to do with her after her mother divorced him, except an occasional call on her birthday or during the holidays.

"I'm not walking away this time, Emma."

He must have moved from the bed toward the door. There was an odd sound to his voice, a thickness, but she didn't want to dwell on what it could be—probably frustration at not being able to control her. Control was paramount to her father. Wasn't that one of the reasons her mother had left him?

A bone-weary exhaustion compelled her to close her eyes, to relax the taut set of her body. It took too much energy to remain on guard. "I don't want you here. Please leave," she murmured through dry lips. She needed water, but she didn't want him to see her try to find the pitcher and plastic cup the nurse had left on the beside table. She couldn't appear helpless in front of him. Strength was the only thing he related to.

"For the moment. But I'll be back, Emma."

The sound of the door closing drew a breath of relief from her. She waited a few minutes, gathering her energy before attempting to get a glass of water. She tried lifting her uninjured arm, but her confrontation with her father had sapped more of her strength than she had thought. Parched, she lay helpless in her bed.

Why is this happening to me?

She wanted to scream and hide at the same time. She wanted to sleep but was afraid the nightmare would return. She wanted to be in control of her life. She wanted her big brother to hold her and tell her everything would be all right. Over the years she had wanted a lot of things, but that didn't—

"Miss St. James?"

She gasped, totally taken by surprise. That thought sent panic through her. So exposed. Alone.

"Colin Fitzpatrick."

"The reverend? Why are you back?" *Please leave me alone. Can't you see I don't want visitors? Can't you see I'm barely holding myself together?*

"I couldn't leave without telling you why I visited in the first place."

There was a long moment of silence that heightened Emma's feeling of vulnerability. She had no idea what was really going on around her.

"I was driving the car that hit you."

"Hit me?" Emma murmured, her forehead wrinkling.

"Last night my SUV struck you on the highway." As that sentence tumbled from his mouth, Colin's guilt prodded him forward toward the woman who looked lost in the hospital bed, as though she was unraveling before his eyes.

"You were there?" Her frown deepened.

"I tried to avoid you. I thought I had. But—" His words died on his lips.

She touched her shoulder where the bandage was. "I thought I was shot." Closing her eyes, she buried her face in her hands.

"You were."

With a shake of her head she looked in his direction. "I'm confused. I wish I remembered what happened. I was shot but you hit me, too?"

Colin nodded, then realized she couldn't see him and said, "Yes."

"Why didn't you tell me that earlier? What kind of game are you playing? Who are you, really?"

The questions lashed out at him, and he took a step back. "I'm exactly who I said I was. I'm a minister. I was driving home from a conference with some members of the youth group at my church when the accident occurred."

"What do you want from me?"

"Nothing."

"Nothing?"

The confused look on her face spoke volumes to him. He wondered about the cynical expression as he said, "I want to help you. I know how hard it is to lose someone you love. I told you earlier that I was a good listener. If I—"

"Please," she interrupted, turning her head away from him. "I just want to be left—"

The door opened. Emma stopped in mid-sentence, the sound prompting her to glance toward the person entering. Colin didn't need any introductions to the older woman making her entrance. Her honey-colored hair fell to her shoulders in thick, lustrous waves, not a hint of gray. Her beautiful, flawless face held no wrinkles, as though time had stopped for her at thirty or she'd had the use of a good plastic surgeon. Her wide, cobalt-blue eyes were full of concern as Marlena Howard walked toward the bed where her daughter lay.

"Emma, I got here as fast as I could, darling."

"Marlena?" Emma blinked. "I thought you were on location."

"Yes, but for you I left. I told the director I would be back when my baby was better." Marlena leaned over and kissed Emma on the cheek. "Just as soon as you can leave, I'll take you home where I can pamper you."

"You know about Derek?"

Tears sprang into Marlena's eyes, slipping down her well-preserved face. "Yes, baby. What you must have gone through." She took her daughter's hand and clasped it between hers. "I don't understand any of this. Who would want to hurt him—or you?"

Emma's lower lip quivered.

"We talked right before I left to shoot the movie. Everything was great."

Colin felt as though he was watching a performance by an accomplished actress and he didn't like that thought. The dutiful sorrow was in the woman's voice, the tears in her eyes, but something was missing. He stepped forward. "I'm Reverend Colin Fitzpatrick."

Marlena focused on him for a few seconds, then shifted to her daughter. "Emma, is there something you aren't telling me? I was assured by your doctor that you would be all right in time."

"I can't see!" A hysterical ring entered Emma's voice. Her teeth bit into her lower lip to still its trembling.

"I know, baby. But the doctor told me there wasn't any physical reason, that with time you'll be as good as new." Marlena glanced around the room. "I can't believe you got the flowers I sent you already. I know lilies are your favorite. I told the florist to fill your room with them."

Colin watched Emma cringe when her mother talked about her blindness. She withdrew further as the older woman chatted as though what had happened to her daughter wasn't that big a deal.

"Those aren't from you, Marlena."

"They aren't? Then who sent them?" A rare wrinkle creased the older woman's brow.

The nurse said the card read "Brandon McDonel."

"Derek's friend?"

"We've dated in the past."

"Who sent you a potted plant?"

"My assistant."

"And the yellow roses?"

"I did."

The deep, booming voice drew everyone's attention toward the door. A tall, commanding figure stood in the entrance, filling it with his powerful presence.

"I'm glad you could pull yourself away from the set to visit our daughter." William St. James entered, making sure the door closed behind him.

Marlena straightened, leveling a narrowed look at the large man making his way to the hospital bed. "*Our* daughter? You gave up that right twenty years ago."

Colin's attention remained on Emma, who pulled the covers up until she was almost hidden beneath them.

"And now that Derek is gone, you want to reclaim what is mine." Marlena's voice vibrated with possession.

Emma averted her face, staring away from her parents. Colin advanced closer, wanting to protect Emma from the two people who should love her the most. They squared off, confronting each other at the end of their daughter's bed. Marlena, not much over five feet, should have been intimidated by William's sheer size of over six and a half feet. She wasn't. She matched him glare for glare.

"Contrary to when she was a little girl, *our* daughter is a grown woman now and can make her own choices." William inched closer to Marlena, his arms rigid at his sides.

"Not while she's sick and vulnerable. I won't let you take advantage of her like that."

A sheen shimmered in Emma's eyes. She squeezed them closed. Colin's heart bled for the woman in the hospital bed, listening to her parents battle over her as though she were a prize in a dogfight.

Colin laid a hand on Emma's shoulder, wanting to convey support. She didn't shrink from his touch. That in itself told him how distraught she was over the scene being played out in her hospital room.

"I can protect her. She's in danger." William's hands bunched into fists.

"I can care for her until she's well. I'm just as capable of hiring a small army to protect my daughter as you are."

Finally, as though she realized he was touching her, Emma shifted away. "Stop it, you two!" Even though the words she uttered were forceful, her hoarse voice came out on a weak thread.

"For how long, Marlena? Until some man catches your fancy? Or a movie you have to star in sends you halfway around the world? What about the one you're working on right now?" Oblivious to his daughter's plea, William uncurled his hands, then knotted them again.

"Jealous I have an exciting life while yours is only filled with boring—"

"Stop it!"

Emma's words swung both her parents around to face her. Side by side, at the end of the bed, they stared at her. Her mother's expressive eyes were huge while her father's veiled his expression.

"I need you all to leave. I won't be in the middle of you two fighting. I'm tired," Emma murmured, her voice growing weaker with each word said. As though to emphasize how exhausted she was, her eyes slid closed and some of her tension siphoned from her.

Marlena frowned, glared at her ex-husband, then nodded toward the door. Colin suspected Emma's mother wanted to resume the argument in the corridor. As she headed toward the door, her jaw set in a determined look while Emma's father finally exhibited some emotion—hatred.

The intense feelings that churned the air in the small hospital room rocked Colin. He wasn't even a member of the family, and he felt weary from the brief skirmish waged in front of him, a stranger. What kind of life had Emma St. James been exposed to while growing up, the daughter of two bitter parents each of whom used her to get to the other one? He'd seen it before, and it often left deep scars in the child caught between two warring parents.

He peered down at Emma, her face finally relaxed as

the silence flowed, chasing away the echoes of her parents' exchange. She was petite like Marlena Howard, but that was where the similar physical attributes ended. Beneath the scratches and bruises on her face, he noted a beautiful woman with long black curly hair and soft brown eyes that spoke of emotions she wished she could control. How similar were they beyond the physical?

He'd accomplished what he had set out to do when he'd come into the room. She knew he had hit her with his car. But there was so much more he wanted—needed—to do. And yet, the closed eyes and motionless body told him she wanted him to leave, too. He moved toward the door, his guilt still bearing down on him. He couldn't blame her for not wanting to talk to him.

He had reached out to grasp the door handle when he heard her say, "Stay, please."

THREE

Emma shifted on the bed, trying to stifle a moan from escaping when pain lanced through her. Her head and shoulder ached and every square inch of her body was sore, as though a herd of elephants had trampled over her. "I'm sorry you had to be a witness to that."

"I'm sorry *you* had to be."

The reverend's voice was a deep baritone, smooth sounding with just a hint of a Southern drawl. What did he look like? She tried to imagine him from the way his voice sounded, but it was useless. He could be twenty-five, forty or sixty. She couldn't tell by the mere sound of his voice. Frustration churned her stomach. As a photographer, her profession centered around the visual, and she had no idea what the man talking to her looked like.

He cleared his throat. "Is there a reason you wanted me to stay?"

Emma heard her mother's voice from the hallway. Heat scored her cheeks as she thought of all the people in the corridor listening to her mother and father fight. Their marriage and breakup—in fact, all her mother's three other ones—had played out in the tabloids, making her promise to herself never to have her life plastered before the public like her mother's. She preferred being behind the camera, not in front.

Emma licked her dry lips and said, "No particular reason. I just—" She couldn't admit to this stranger that she'd had a sudden fear of being left alone with only darkness around her. She'd always been afraid of the dark and now she lived in it. A tremor of alarm quaked through her.

His footsteps approaching the bed made her tense, her fingernails digging into her palms. The scraping of a chair nearby echoed through her mind, ridiculing her with how helpless she was, lying in this bed.

"I'll stay as long as you want me to."

Kindness coated his words, causing a spurt of anger to well inside her. "To appease your guilty conscience?"

"Yes and no," he replied slowly as though considering his answer carefully. "I tried to avoid you on the highway, but you spun into my path. That's something I'll have to live with."

"No, that's something *I'll* have to live with." She wasn't quite ready to let go of her anger—not necessarily directed at the man beside her bed.

He released a long sigh. "I'm here because I sense you need someone to talk to."

Regretting her words, she closed her eyes and searched her mind for any hint of what had happened the night before. Nothing. All she could recall about yesterday was driving from New York, the wind blowing through her hair, the sun beating down on her. She'd felt free, escaping the hectic pace of her life as a photographer to the stars, thrust into the limelight almost as much as the people she took pictures of. She'd spent the whole day enjoying being by herself for once. That was why she had chosen to drive instead of fly. Now all she sought was *not* to be by herself—alone with her thoughts, her fears, her grief.

"When I was shot—" She touched her bandaged shoulder, still shocked at the turn of events.

"Yes?"

His gentle voice, sprinkled with the Southern drawl, urged her to talk. "The sheriff told me they don't have any leads. You didn't see anyone?"

"No. I understand from the sheriff that you don't remember what happened."

"Nothing." Tears that were so close to the surface sprang into her eyes. "The police think I might have seen something, but what good is it? I don't remember." The throbbing in her head intensified with each effort to recall what had happened. She massaged her temples, rubbed her sightless eyes.

"Sometimes it's best not to push it. Your memory will come back when you're ready."

"If I saw something to help—" Her tears strangled the flow of words, her mouth as arid as Death Valley.

She swallowed several times, and still she couldn't finish what she'd wanted to say. Wet tracks coursed down her face. She swiped at them, turning away from the stranger sitting next to her. The tight lump in her throat made it impossible to get a decent breath.

He placed his hand over hers. "Your mind's blocking the memories for a reason. Concentrate on getting well instead of remembering. It'll come when you're ready to handle it."

The feel of his touch centered her. She inhaled deeply

until her lungs were full of rich oxygen and her heart returned to a normal beat.

For a long moment silence reigned. Emma noticed that her parents' voices couldn't be heard anymore. Relief flowed through her like a river swollen with rainwater. She couldn't deal with them right now. In the past it had taken so much of her emotional strength to handle the conflicting feelings surrounding her parents. She loved her mother, but the great Marlena Howard drained her emotionally.

And your father? an inner voice asked. She didn't know what she felt for her father. He'd left when she was eight. Memories of loud fighting and slamming doors inundated her. She shoved those away before they overpowered her.

The reverend's hand over hers squeezed gently. "You need time to heal."

Emma drew in a deep breath. The broken pieces of her life lay scattered about her. Heal? Where did she start? She expelled her breath slowly between pursed lips. "There's so much that's happened." She faltered at the vulnerability that sounded in her voice. She didn't know this man. Always before she'd held herself apart from others. So much was shifting, altering what was her life. How was she going to proceed without her dear brother, without her sight, her work? That was what defined her.

"When life seems overwhelming, I find it's best to think only of the immediate present."

"Take it one day at a time?"

"I know it's a cliché, but it's good advice."

His hand slipped away and for a brief moment she

wanted to snatch it back, to clasp it and never let it go. A lifeline? Panic began to nibble at her brittle composure. She didn't depend on anyone—hadn't since—

"When are you leaving the hospital?"

She grasped on to the reverend's question, turning her thoughts away from that past best forgotten, from that looming future. "The doctor said I can go home tomorrow." Home? Where was that? Her apartment in New York? Her mother's? She shook. She clenched her hands to keep them from trembling.

"Then you'll be leaving Crystal Springs tomorrow?"

"No," she said without thinking, the word wrenched from the depth of her being. The pounding in her head magnified tenfold. "I don't know what I'm going to be doing."

"You shouldn't be alone."

"That's what my father and mother say, but I can't go with either one of them. They'll make me feel like a rope in a tug-of-war game."

"Where do you live?"

"I have an apartment in Manhattan."

"Is there anyone who can stay with you?"

Emma thought of her so-called friends and couldn't think of a single person she would want to ask. She'd always been a private person who traveled a lot for her work. It had been difficult to maintain friendships, especially when she found so many people only wanted to get to know her because of her parents. She worked and lived with many people around her, but they were really only acquaintances or employees. Suddenly, the lonely existence of her life taunted her.

"No, there isn't anyone I could ask." She didn't want to go to New York and be subjected to her acquaintances' pitying looks, which she wouldn't be able to see. The idea of holing herself up in her apartment didn't appeal to her, either. "I don't know what I'm going to do after I leave the hospital."

"And your parents aren't an option."

"You've got that right." It hadn't really been a question, but she answered anyway, needing to emphasize to herself how impossible it would be to live with either of her parents while recovering. "You saw them. Neither one's thinking about Derek, about—" Emotions she didn't want to feel swelled into her throat, knotting her words into a huge ball. Her older brother had been the one person she could turn to when she needed advice, a friendly ear who hadn't wanted something from her. She couldn't imagine life without him. Didn't want to think about it.

Tears returned. She rolled onto her side away from the Reverend Colin Fitzpatrick. One tear then another slipped from her eyes. It was so much easier not to think, not to feel.

"Emma?"

"I'm tired, Reverend. I'm sure there are others who need you more than I do." *It's too late to help me,* she thought, pressing her lips together to keep the words inside.

Her tough words did nothing to disguise the sob in her voice. Wanting to comfort, Colin started to reach for her, but hesitated. If her stiff back and averted face were any indication, she didn't want it. And he wouldn't add to her pain. He'd done enough already.

"I'll be back," he murmured as he walked toward the door, determined somehow to help the woman he'd hit.

He paused outside her room, taking a moment to get his bearings and decide what to do next. The sound of her cries could be heard through the door. His chest tightened with sorrow. There was a part of him that needed to go back into her room and hold her, give her what solace he could, but he also knew she needed time to grieve by herself. She was a loner who he was sure had shown more emotion today to him than she usually did to people she knew.

He understood all too well what she was going through. He'd lost his wife several years before and the pain was gut-wrenching. It had taken time for him to turn to others for help. He had to respect that, but he wanted to be there when Emma needed it. He owed her.

Dear Heavenly Father, watch over Emma St. James. Soothe her pain and help her to accept Your grace and love. She will need them in the days to come.

With reluctance Colin headed for the bank of elevators. He needed to talk with J.T. and find out what the sheriff knew so far with this case.

Fifteen minutes later Colin stood in the middle of J.T.'s office, facing the sheriff. "Any leads?"

J.T.'s dark, assessing gaze zeroed in on Colin. "Not much to go on. The cabin was obviously searched. We got a tire print at the cabin and footprints from the side of the road where they shot her. That's all at the moment."

"They? There was more than one killer?"

"From the footprints that's a strong possibility. Did she remember anything after I left?"

Colin shook his head. "Did you talk with her doctor?"

"Yes, with her permission."

His heartbeat sped up, his palms sweaty. He had to ask and yet he didn't want to know. "Why can't she see?" *Did I do that to her when I hit her?*

"There isn't a physical reason. It's all psychological, according to the doctor. She'll see when she's ready."

"What in the world did she witness that she refuses to remember? Her brother's murder?"

"Probably."

"Do you think she's in danger?"

"Could be. Then again, whoever killed Derek could be long gone, especially if they were hired to do the job or if they were just looking for something of value to steal. It doesn't look like anything was stolen, but then we really don't know for sure what Derek St. James had with him. We may never know."

"She's leaving the hospital tomorrow."

J.T. straightened in his chair. "Where's she going?"

"She doesn't know."

"I'd rather her not leave town, but there's really nothing I can do to stop her."

"I don't want her going back to Manhattan and being alone in her apartment."

"Especially if someone thinks she witnessed what happened to her brother and wants to eliminate her. Do you have any suggestions for her?"

Colin kneaded the back of his neck, an idea taking form. "Maybe. But first I need to talk to someone. I'll let you know what my aunt says."

"Grace." J.T. laughed. "That tough old cookie."

"Don't let my aunt hear you call her old."

J.T. scratched his jaw. "And if she finds out, I'll know who told her."

"Your secret is safe with me as long as you keep me informed of any progress with the case."

"So you've taken a personal interest in this murder."

"It's definitely personal. A woman's lying in a hospital bed because of me."

"No, not because of you."

"I didn't help the situation by hitting her with my car. She's going to be sore a long time because of me."

"But she's alive. Did you ever think that if you hadn't happened along at the time you did, she would be dead right now?"

Colin frowned. "That should comfort me, but it doesn't. It was hard watching her try to remember and deal with not being able to."

J.T. rose. "She'll be mighty lucky to have you and Grace watching over her."

"She may not think so. You know how my aunt can be."

"Yup. She doesn't take no for an answer and has the strength and will to back it up."

"But she'll be a good bodyguard when I'm not around."

"So that's what this is all about?"

"Someone needs to watch over Emma St. James and I believe the Lord picked me when my SUV hit her. I may be a bit rusty, but I know how." His Special Forces training might help someone after all these years.

Colin left the sheriff's office and headed toward home, eager to see his aunt now that he had a plan to keep Emma safe until her memory returned—until he had repaid his debt to her. When he pulled into his driveway, he saw Grace's Jeep Cherokee parked at the side of her house, which was next door to his. Glad to see she was home, he hopped from his vehicle and hurried across his lawn.

Even though he had a key to his aunt's house, he didn't use it. Instead, he pressed the bell and waited for her to open the door.

Dressed in army fatigues with her short red hair spiked on top, Grace blocked his entrance into her foyer. "I wondered when you'd come visit me. I heard about your little trouble last night." Finally she stepped aside to allow him into her house.

"Been busy with the sheriff and visiting the woman at the hospital."

"Emma St. James?"

He nodded and started toward his aunt's kitchen. He needed a large cup of coffee if he was going to keep himself going.

"I also heard her mother is in town. Staying at the inn near the lake."

"Is there anything you *don't* hear, Grace?" His aunt was only ten years older than he and when she'd come to live in Crystal Springs after her retirement from the military she had insisted he call her only Grace. He'd learned early on never to disobey her, so Grace it was.

"Not much. You've got to know what's going on. That way no one can take you by surprise."

In the kitchen Colin poured himself some of the coffee that was always on the stove in his aunt's house. She lived on the stuff and yet slept like a baby at night. "Well, Ms. St. James took me by surprise last night. She came out of the woods and straight at my car."

"Sugar, I've got to teach you some defensive driving."

Colin gripped his mug. "I swerved, but so did she."

Grace eased her slender body into a chair at the oak table and pulled her coffee cup closer. "Sometimes there's nothing a person can do to avoid an accident. Don't beat yourself up over it. That's wasted energy, and you know how I am about wasted energy."

Sitting across from his aunt, Colin took a large swallow of the warm brew, relishing its strong taste. He and his aunt had similar tastes when it came to coffee. "I have a favor to ask." He fastened his attention on his aunt. "Emma needs a place to stay for a while."

"She can stay here."

"First, Grace, you should know that she may have seen the killers and they may be after her."

"No problem. I spent years teaching recruits how to protect themselves. I think I can protect one woman."

"Are you sure?" He had to ask. He didn't want his aunt not to know she could be in danger even though he knew she could take care of herself, better than most men.

"Never been a bodyguard. Maybe I should take up a second profession. Yes, sugar, I'm sure. Emma St. James is in trouble and the good Lord taught us to help our neighbors in need. That's all I'm doing."

The tension inside him melted some with his aunt's words. All his life he had looked up to her and had even followed in her footsteps by going into the army. And her strong faith in God had been the guiding force behind him becoming a Christian and turning his life's work over to the Lord.

"So what's this Emma St. James look like? Anything like her mother? I'm a big fan of Marlena Howard."

"No, I'd say she looks more like her father—long, curly dark hair and big chocolate-colored eyes."

"Chocolate-colored? Sugar, what kind of description is that?"

Colin chuckled. "The kind a man who's hungry would say."

Grace scooted the chair back and stood. "What do you want for lunch?" She started for the refrigerator, adding, "When's she coming to stay here?"

"That, Grace, hasn't been decided, since I still have to ask her if she wants to stay in Crystal Springs to recuperate."

Sweat poured off Roy as he reached for the phone to put in the call he had dreaded making for the past twenty-four hours. Punching the number into the pay phone, he tugged at the blue cotton material of the shirt that stuck to his skin.

Ring.

Roy's heart hammered a fast tempo inside his head. His mouth went dry.

Ring.

Sweat rolled in his eyes, stinging them.

Ring.

Roy had started to hang up when a frosty voice said, "Hello."

The slick, wet feel of the receiver turned ice-cold in his hand. "Roy here, reporting in."

"All I want to know is how are you going to fix this little problem."

It wasn't the words that bothered Roy, but the way his employer on the other end said them—with such coldness that Roy felt the menacing threat even though they weren't in the same room. "I'm on it, boss."

"You are?"

Sarcasm with a hint of amusement encased him in fear. "She doesn't remember anything, and on top of that, she can't see a thing."

"That could change."

"Do you want me to take care of her?"

There was a long pause on the other end. Roy envisioned his employer frowning, icy eyes narrowed on a point across the room while his employer was deep in thought.

"No, not yet. Another murder could have everything blowing up in our faces. Bring me the packet and you two disappear."

Roy's heart stopped beating for a painful few seconds, his breath trapped in his lungs.

"Roy, what aren't you telling me?"

"Manny and me didn't get the papers. We didn't have time to search the cabin thoroughly."

"So they're still at the cabin?"

"I think so."

"You think so?"

"Derek never said where they was. He wasn't gonna talk. But I believe he brought them with him when he came to Crystal Springs. They're at that cabin somewhere, hidden so well the sheriff hasn't found them."

"But you don't know for sure?"

The lethal edge to his employer's words cut through Roy, leaving him shaking in his boots. "As soon as the sheriff is through with the cabin, we'll search it until we find what you need."

"You better. And keep me posted on Emma St. James."

"Will do." Roy quickly hung up, his hand trembling

so badly he dropped the receiver into its cradle, its loud sound snaking down his spine.

Emma felt the warmth of the sunshine as it flooded the room and slanted across her bed. Earlier she'd heard the nurse opening the curtain and had wondered why the woman even bothered, because it didn't make any difference whether there was light in the room or not. But she hadn't voiced her thought aloud.

As with the day before, darkness greeted her. To keep her panic at bay she kept her eyes closed, pretending the darkness was due to that rather than the fact she couldn't see anymore. She didn't like pity parties and had never allowed herself one. But then she had never been blind before, either. She'd never lost the one person who had understood her, accepted her for who she was.

Clasping the sides of her head, she shuddered. "Don't go there, Emma. Not a good place." Another shudder trembled through her body, leaving a coldness in its wake.

The door swishing open intruded into her thoughts, bringing her straight up in bed to turn her face toward the noise. "Who is it?" She couldn't shake the idea she could be a target. Even though she had bravely told her father the day before that she could take care of herself, she had her doubts.

"Colin Fitzpatrick."

The tension siphoned from her at the velvet smoothness of his voice as though he could mesmerize a person with its mere sound. "Nothing's changed. I'm past saving."

"No one's past saving if she wants to be saved."

"I don't know if I agree with you, but come on in since you're here." The idea that she didn't have to spend the next few minutes alone lifted her spirits. But she wasn't ready to admit it to anyone, especially Reverend Colin Fitzpatrick. "What brings you by?"

"You."

His answer made her spirits rise even more, and she didn't understand why. She leaned toward the sound of his voice. "I'm getting out of here later this afternoon. I get to escape all the poking and prodding."

"Where are you going when you escape?"

"Haven't the faintest idea. Any suggestions?"

"Actually, I do."

His words took her by surprise and that didn't happen very often. "Where?" she asked, a breathless quality to her voice, her mouth and throat still so parched she felt she'd eaten a bowl of cotton for lunch.

"My aunt's. She has extended an invitation for you to stay with her."

"Why? She doesn't know me."

"I asked her to."

"Why?"

"I don't want you to be alone right now."

"Do you think I'm helpless?"

"No."

"Do you think I'm in danger?"

"It's a possibility and my aunt can certainly take care of you."

"Is she with the police?"

"She's retired from the army, but her last job was teaching people how to defend themselves."

When he had said retired, a vision of a woman in her

sixties or seventies, white haired, bent over, popped into Emma's mind. Even if his aunt had taught self-defense and had been in the army, she was hardly someone who could take care of her. "How old is she?"

"Forty-six."

"And she's retired?"

"Only from the army. She writes children's books now."

Conflicting images flowed through her mind—none of them of someone who she thought could protect her. "If your aunt's forty-six, how old are you? Twenty?"

"Thirty-six, so she's more like a big sister than an aunt, and she won't let me call her Aunt Grace. Just Grace."

His answer sent relief through her and she wasn't sure why. "I still don't understand how a stranger would want to help me."

"You'll understand when you meet Grace. My daughters practically live over at her house. They think she's cool."

"Daughters? You're married?" Of course, he would be. Why would she think otherwise and why had she bothered to ask?

"My wife died four years ago. I have fifteen-year-old twins who have tested this father's patience on more than one occasion."

Exasperation roughened his voice, masking his Southern drawl. Emma laughed. "That's what teenage girls are put on this earth for."

"To test fathers' patience?"

"To be exasperating." Memories of her own father, absent from her teenage years, flooded her mind and all laughter faded.

"Then they have fulfilled their calling. So what do

you say? Want to spend some time in Crystal Springs recovering?"

Thinking about the blank pages of her mind chilled her to the marrow of her bones. Whom should she trust?

FOUR

Emma grasped Colin's elbow and allowed him to lead her to his aunt's porch. On the last step, Emma's foot caught and she stumbled forward. Colin caught her before she fell flat on her face. She gritted her teeth, feeling the heat of embarrassment scorching her cheeks. The simple act of walking was even difficult now. Ever since she'd left her hospital room twenty minutes ago, she felt as though she were Alice in Wonderland, nothing as it seemed and everything different.

"Okay?"

His concern brought her anger to the foreground. "I'm just great. I love being led around like a child." The second she said that last sentence, she sensed Colin stiffen beside her.

He proceeded forward, his arm still wrapped about her. She stepped away. For a few seconds she stood alone, not sure what lay in front or to the side. Her vulnerability increased, making a mockery of her sense of independence, something she had always been proud of and had desperately needed. No more. She had to depend on others—virtual strangers—and she wasn't sure how she would cope. But staying with her mother or father had not been an option.

"I'm sorry. I shouldn't have said that. You've done more than enough for me. Any person who can avoid the press as you did at the hospital has my debt of gratitude."

"I know all the ways into the hospital. They don't. It was a piece of cake."

"It won't be long before they figure out where I am. Are you ready for them?"

"They haven't met my aunt. She'll take care of them."

The chimes of the bell announced their arrival and caused Emma to wonder again at the decision she'd made in the hospital. Having no one really to turn to was a sad statement on her life. Until now, she hadn't even realized how isolated she was from others.

A good minute later the door opened. The scents of apples and cinnamon wafted to Emma, causing her mouth to water. She inhaled a deep breath of the delicious smells, her appetite aroused for the first time in days.

"You must be Emma St. James," a woman said in a voice that was loud and commanding with a thick Southern drawl.

A hand larger than hers took hold of Emma's and pumped her arm in a vigorous handshake.

"I'm Colin's aunt, Grace. Come in. Come in."

The woman clasped her and pulled her into the house. Emma thought of a steamroller barreling over her. Her mind spun, her senses assaulted with so much unfamiliarity. The unknown, in more ways than one, lay before her and a panicky feeling grew.

"I'm finishing up in the kitchen. Colin, bring her on in while I take the pies out of the oven."

His aunt released her grip on Emma. Grace's footsteps sounded on the hardwood floor as she hurried away.

He shifted toward her. "Here, take my arm."

Emma froze. Her mind continued to reel with sensations, smells and sounds coming at her from all sides, overloading her. A clock ticked to the right of her while gospel music played in the background. Infused in the scents of cinnamon and apples was a lemony odor with a faint hint of bleach. Chimes noting the hour of two blared through the din.

"Emma?" Colin's gentle voice added to all the other noises bombarding her.

"Stop." She shook her head, backing up a pace. "I can't do this." Her impulse was to turn around and flee, then the reality of her situation gripped her and she knew she wouldn't be going anywhere. She didn't even know where the door was!

"I'm sorry. I can show you to your room, instead. Grace will understand."

Will she? I don't. "Please. I'm tired." She winced at the weak thread to her words, but feelings of hopelessness and helplessness assailed her, pressing her down into a black void she was afraid she would never emerge from.

He gave her his arm again, then began plodding forward, one slow step at a time. "Grace has fixed up a bedroom in the back on the first floor. That way you don't—"

"Have to break my neck on the stairs," she said, thinking of the near accident on the porch.

"Well, maybe that, too. But what I was going to say is that you don't have to learn the layout of the second story."

Learn the layout? The realization she would have to

fumble her way around the house or have someone lead her made her want to escape to her room, pull the covers over her head and never come out.

They stopped. She heard the sound of a door creaking open.

"I'll oil the hinges," Colin said, going ahead of her into the bedroom, then guiding her through the entrance.

"Don't."

He chuckled. "I guess it's a pretty effective way of telling if someone comes into your room."

His laugh was infectious, the sound almost shoving her melancholy mood to the background. "I'm going to need all the help I can get."

"Let me start by describing this room. I'll help you pace it off, too."

"You sound like you've had experience with this."

Even though she couldn't see his expression, she knew he was frowning. Tension emanated off him in waves. Silence electrified the air, and his touch tightened for a few seconds before his fingers relaxed about hers. Her natural curiosity arose, and she wondered about the man who had taken her into his family. All she knew was his kindness and his gentle, deep voice. And the warmth of his touch, she added as he moved forward.

"We'll count off from the door to the bed. Ready?"

She nodded, following his lead and listening to him as he counted the steps to the bed.

"Seven. There's a bathroom off this room. Do you want to see how far that is?"

She liked that he was giving her a choice, giving her a tiny bit of power in her life, which at the moment seemed so out of her control. Ever since the one time she'd lost control, it had been important she maintained it. She didn't want to relive those feelings of a few years ago. "Yes, please."

Again she walked across the room with Colin plastered next to her. He was a large man and from the brief time he had taken hold of her to keep her from falling she could tell that he was muscularly built if his arms and chest were any indication of the rest of him.

"Five." Standing in the doorway to the bathroom, he said, "The counter is to the left. You can slide your hand along it and the toilet is right next to it with the tub on the other side. You want to try it?"

Emma felt the smoothness of the door frame then the cool tile of the counter. Slipping her fingers along it, she encountered the sink then the end. She inched one foot forward until she discovered the toilet. Then sidling in front of it, she found the tub. After exploring the bathroom for a few minutes, she fumbled her way back to its entrance.

Colin offered her his arm.

"No. I want to do it on my own. Five steps to the bed."

She started forward, counting to herself. Her shins tingled with anticipation of running into an obstacle. When she reached three, she held her arms out in front of her to search for the bed. At five she bumped into it. She groped along until she came to the left-side corner, then turned and walked toward what she hoped was the doorway into the bedroom, counting off seven paces. Again she expected to run into something with every step she took, making her movements stiff and awkward, conjuring up an image of Dr. Frankenstein's monster from an old movie she'd seen once. She didn't care what she must look like because she was determined to master this room, *today*.

When she grasped the wooden door frame, she sank against it, dragging in deep breaths. Exhaustion wrapped about her like a heavy wet blanket, pulling her down.

"Do you want to rest for a while before I show you the rest of the downstairs?"

His gentle voice coming at her from a few feet away startled her. She hadn't been listening for his approach, which was muffled by the thick carpet. Her vulnerability mushroomed, constricting her chest until it hurt. Again, that panicky feeling clawed at her composure.

"I'm sorry, Emma. I didn't mean to scare you."

She pushed herself away from the door frame. "At the hospital you said my luggage and car were delivered here."

"The car is parked in back and your suitcase is on the bed. J.T. had to tow the car here."

"Why? My keys should be in my purse. Where is it?"

A long moment of silence filled the room before Colin replied, "I don't know. J.T. didn't bring it with your other things."

"He didn't find it?" Her voice rose with thoughts of Derek's killer going through her handbag, learning all kinds of personal information about her.

"I'll check with him and see. But there shouldn't have been any reason for him to keep it. Where was it? In the car?"

Emma searched the blank corners of her mind but couldn't remember where her purse had been last. She muttered the words she had spoken too much lately, "I don't know."

"I'll let J.T. know. You'll probably want to cancel your credit cards."

"I only have one, and I can call my business manager to take care of that."

"There's a phone on the left side table by the bed. Grace won't mind if you call. Do you want me to dial the number?"

"No," she replied with more force than she intended. She was going to do what she could by herself even if it took a while.

Remembering the number of steps, Emma made her way to the bed, a little more confident in what she was doing. She fumbled until her hand encountered the phone, then running the tips of her fingers along the buttons, after several tries, she finally placed the call to Adam Moore.

Five minutes later, she hung up from talking with her business manager and accountant, relieved not to answer any more of his questions. Even though she was weary, she turned in Colin's direction and said, "Tell me about this room. What else is in here besides this bed and bedside table?"

He came to her and faced the same direction she was, as though putting himself in her shoes, his arm brushing against hers. "This is a large bedroom with plenty of space to move about. You know where the king-sized bed is. There's an end table with a lamp on the other side, too. Behind the bedside tables are two small windows that face the south. Across from the end of the bed is a chest of drawers. To its right is a lounge chair. The closet is two feet from the bathroom to the right."

"I want to walk the perimeter." Emma took his upper arm on his left side so she could feel the pieces of furniture as they circled the room.

"Are you sure you don't want to rest first?"

"No!" Her body ached with fatigue, her shoulder throbbing, but she wouldn't lie down until she knew every inch of her bedroom.

"Is she settled in?" Grace asked, pouring herself a cup of coffee then Colin one.

"She's finally resting." Colin took the mug and sat at the kitchen table. "Any chance I can get a piece of apple pie?" He looked toward the counter where the dessert was cooling on a rack. The smells of cinnamon and apple still peppered the air, stirring his hunger. "I didn't eat lunch."

"Then I'll fix you a sandwich. Sugar, you know apple pie shouldn't be your lunch."

"Grace, Grace, you need to give up trying to reform me. I have a sweet tooth and that isn't gonna change."

"Yes, and all the women of the congregation know it and make a point of supplying you with plenty of sweets, including me. Who do you think I was baking these for? Certainly not myself." She tsked, her mouth twisting into a wry grin. "I don't know how you stay so trim."

"I do follow your advice about working out. So I'm not a total lost cause."

She peered heavenward. "Thankfully I've done something right." She went to the refrigerator and retrieved the makings of a turkey sandwich.

"You've done a lot right. I thank the Lord every day that you are in my life. And my girls feel the same way."

"Speaking of Amber and Tiffany, they should be here soon." Grace glanced at the rooster clock over the stove. "School was out a half hour ago."

Not three minutes later, as his aunt cut his sandwich in two, the doorbell rang. He shot to his feet and said, "I'll get it."

He hurried into the foyer and thrust the door open before Tiffany had a chance to ring the bell again. She charged into the house with Amber following at a more sedate pace. They dropped their backpacks on the floor and headed straight for the kitchen.

Colin trailed after his daughters, glancing toward the bedroom where Emma slept before entering the kitchen. "And a good day to you both."

"Sorry, Dad. I'm starved. I could smell Aunt Grace's pie out on the lawn." Tiffany took a plate down from the cabinet and sliced into the pie.

"Hey, did you have lunch today?"

Tiffany, the older of the two by four minutes, threw him a quizzical look. "Of course, Dad. I don't skip lunch like *some* of us in the room." Her narrowed eyes zoomed in on him.

He shrugged. "I've been busy."

Amber plopped down at the kitchen table with a tall glass of iced tea. "How is she?"

Seated across from his subdued, quiet daughter, he answered, "Miss St. James is doing as well as to be expected."

"When do we get to meet her? I can't believe Marlena Howard's daughter is staying here!" Tiffany joined them at the table with her huge piece of pie and a generous scoop of vanilla ice cream.

"Child, you definitely take after your father. You must have a hollow leg, too." Grace busied cleaning up after the whirlwind known as Tiffany.

"I'm on the track team."

"Ah, that must be it. You're skinny as a rail." Grace sat in the last chair across from Amber.

Colin noticed Amber studying her glass as though it had a written message on it. Unlike Tiffany, Amber put on weight easily and was carrying an extra fifteen pounds. She was constantly dieting but rarely losing. Although they were identical twins, Amber and Tiffany were like night and day. They even wore their dark brown hair differently, with Amber's long and pulled back into a ponytail most of the time while Tiffany's was short and feathered about her face, emphasizing her large gray eyes.

"Dad, when can we meet her?" Tiffany asked, not forgetting what she really wanted to know. "I've read about her in *People* magazine. She knows a lot of movie stars. She takes all their photos. She's as famous as they are."

"You'll meet her when she's ready. Not a moment sooner, so don't you go charging in there like you own this house."

"But, Daddy—"

"Don't use that with me. It won't work. I only get 'Daddy' when you're trying to wheedle something out of me." It took a supreme effort to keep from smiling at Tiffany. She had him wrapped around her finger and they both knew it. But not this time. Emma needed to move at her own pace. And she certainly didn't need to be caught up in the drama that usually followed Tiffany around like a lost puppy.

A crashing sound disturbed the quiet. Rising, Colin rushed from the kitchen, hoping that Emma was all right. He found her in the hallway outside her bedroom, standing next to a vase smashed into pieces on the hardwood floor. As she stared at her shoes, confusion and frustration washed over her features. He strode forward, stepping around the shards shattered into many fragments about Emma. She looked up. Her eyes shone with unshed tears and his heart cracked.

"I—" She cleared her throat and continued, "I didn't mean to break it." Her forehead furrowed deeper into a frown. "What did I break?"

His first impulse was to take her into his embrace and hold her tight to him, to ease her hurt, more of the soul than anything else. But instinctively he knew she would reject it and her anger would surge to the foreground.

"It's nothing." He stopped in front of her and bent to clean up the pieces of the vase Amber had made for Grace last Christmas.

"It didn't sound like nothing. It sounded big. What was it?"

"A vase."

"Valuable?"

"No, not in so many words."

"I can write a check for whatever the cost was. I can at least replace it."

He put the broken pieces on the table. "No need."

"Yes, there's a need. I can pay whatever it takes to replace it."

The frantic ring to her words riveted his full attention to Emma. Her bottom lip quivered as she blinked to rid her eyes of the tears. "There's no price because my daughter made the vase in ceramics class for Grace."

"Oh, it's worse than I thought." She averted her face, swiping her hand across her cheeks.

"It was an accident, Emma. Nothing more, nothing less. Amber will understand and so will Grace. I talked with the sheriff. J.T. told me your purse wasn't anywhere around the cabin or the grounds. They searched the woods between the highway to Central City and the cabin and only found your other shoe."

"Then the murderer has my purse," she murmured, her eyes clouding.

"Probably."

With his confirmation Emma grimaced as though the idea had finally sunk in.

"Do you want to meet my daughters? They're in the kitchen," he said, wanting to take her mind off what had happened at the cabin, at least for a few minutes.

Her chest expanded with a deep breath. "I don't—"

"Please. They would love to meet you." He sensed she had spent enough time alone and needed to be around people to divert her thoughts.

"Okay. I need to apologize to Grace and Amber."

Colin started to tell her she didn't, then realized it would help ease Emma's guilt over the vase. "Then let's count the steps from the doorway of your bedroom to the kitchen. I'll have the table removed today so you don't have to worry about any obstacles in the hallway."

"You don't have to."

"No, but I will."

"I need to learn to maneuver around objects and furniture."

"There'll be plenty of time for that." He started toward the kitchen, counting the steps out loud.

Twelve paces later Colin swung the door open. Then he counted off from the entrance to the table. "Amber and Tiffany, this is Emma St. James." With his daughters saying hi, he pulled out a chair and put Emma's hand on its back. As she sat, he continued, "Amber is on your left, Tiffany is across from you and Grace is on your right."

Before the teenage girls could ask any questions, Grace said, "Sugar, are you all right? We heard something break. You didn't hurt yourself, did you?"

"Just a bruised ego. I'm discovering I can't do much on my own and, for someone who is very independent, that's hard to swallow."

"Put your faith in the Lord. He'll see you through." Grace stood. "Do you want something to eat or drink?"

Colin noticed the tightening about Emma's mouth at the mention of the Lord. A lost sheep, he thought and wondered if that was one of the reasons God had put her in the path of his car the other night.

"No, thank you. I'm not hungry."

"You look different from the pictures I've seen," Tiffany said, drawing Emma's attention to his oldest daughter.

Colin shook his head, trying to get Tiffany's attention. She purposefully ignored him, settling her chin in her palm, her elbow on the table as she leaned toward Emma with the determination to discover whatever she could about the woman.

"I can just imagine. I usually straighten this mess of curls. Haven't had a chance lately, and I'm wearing my hair longer now."

"You have met some really famous people. Can you tell us—"

Colin gave up the indirect approach and said, "Tiffany, that's enough. I believe you've got some homework to do." He hoped his features were arranged in a stern enough expression to convey his intent.

"Not much, Daddy. Really. I—"

"Tiffany!"

"Oh, all right. Fine." She pushed to her feet, peering at Amber. "Coming?"

She rose.

"Amber, I need to talk to you for a sec." Emma shifted her attention to his quiet younger daughter, whose eyes widened at the mention of her name.

"Yes?" Amber mumbled, shock still on her face.

"I'm afraid I ran into the table in the hallway and broke the vase you made for your aunt. Is there any way I can make it up to you or you, Grace?"

"That's okay. Accidents happen." Grace put one of the apple pies into a plastic container for Tiffany to take home.

"Are you sure?"

"Yes, Miss St. James. Aunt Grace is right. I can make another one for her. Don't worry about it." Amber's words rushed out until she ended in a breathless gasp.

Tiffany went racing out of the kitchen when the doorbell rang. "I'll get it," she called from the hallway.

"Are you two sure there isn't anything I can do?"

Both Grace and Amber answered at the same time, "Yes."

The kitchen door swung open and Tiffany, wearing a huge grin, entered with Marlena Howard right behind her.

Before anyone could say anything, Emma's mother

swept across the room, saying, "Darling, I was frantic when the hospital staff told me you'd left. Thankfully, that kind nurse told me where you'd gone."

Emma tensed. "Mother, what are you doing here?"

"I came to take you home."

Tiffany put the pie container on the counter and relaxed against it while Amber sidled toward her. Colin tried to catch Tiffany's attention, but she again refused to look his way. Instead, she stared with adoring eyes at Emma's mother, a silly grin still on her face.

"I'm staying with Grace."

"You can't! They aren't family."

Emma clamped her teeth together to keep from saying what she really wanted to say. Family had never mattered much before to her mother, so why did it now? "Mother, you won't change my mind."

The sound of feet shuffling and a chair scraping across the floor emphasized Emma's disadvantage. She didn't really know what was going on. She felt as though every eye in the room was on her, and she avoided the limelight whenever she could, which was nearly impossible with the parents she had.

"Would you like something to drink? Water?" Grace asked.

"No, no, I'll be all right in a moment."

Her mother's answer sent Emma's blood boiling. No doubt Marlena Howard had put on a performance for the Fitzpatricks. She was so good at that. "Mother, you won't get your way. I'm staying here."

"Excuse me. Emma, my daughters and I need to leave," Colin said.

"I'll walk y'all to the door," Grace said.

The idea of her being alone with her mother compelled Emma to say, "Don't leave. Mother isn't staying, and I still have some things to talk to you about, Colin." If she could have seen Colin, she would have grabbed his hand to keep him in the room. Instead, all she saw was a black void, and when she thought about it, panic overwhelmed her. She experienced that out-of-control feeling she went to great lengths to avoid.

"Fine, but my two daughters have homework that needs to be done, *now*."

By his emphasis on the word *now,* Emma was sure there was a silent message being passed between father and daughters.

"Do I have to?"

That was Tiffany, Emma thought. Her voice was bold, full of confidence, while her sister's wasn't.

"Yes, you have to."

"Then can I have your autograph?"

"Tiffany Fitzpatrick! This isn't the time or the place."

"But, Daddy—"

"Go."

Emma hid her smile behind her hand. The sound of the door swinging closed followed the stomping footsteps across the kitchen.

"I'm sorry about that," Colin said, exasperation in his voice.

"That's okay." Emma sensed Colin sitting down at the table, and relief trembled through her. She wouldn't be alone to face her mother. Normally it wasn't a problem, but she felt at such a disadvantage.

"What are you going to do about Derek's funeral? Are you going?" her mother asked in the heavy silence.

Emma stiffened, clenching her hands in her lap. "Of course I am. Why would you think otherwise?"

"What am I to think? You don't want to have anything to do with me."

Patience, Emma thought and waited a full ten seconds before saying, "I'm sorry you feel that way. I'm doing what I need to do for myself."

"How are you getting to the funeral?"

Emma glanced down, not sure how to answer her. The silence in the room lengthened until her nerves stretched to their limit.

"I'm taking her."

She swung her attention toward Colin. "You don't have to. He'll be buried outside Central City. I can take a cab or something—"

"No, I want to."

"How can you be so unfeeling, Emma? Grace, do you have anything strong to drink?" her mother asked in the melodramatic voice Emma knew too well.

"Coffee and iced tea are all I have besides water."

Her mother huffed and must have stood up, from the sound the chair made across the tile. "I can tell when I'm not wanted. I'll be at the inn for another night, and after the funeral tomorrow, I'm going back to the set."

Her mother's angry footsteps grated down Emma's spine as Grace showed Marlena out. Emma let the quiet extend for a few seconds before she said, "I'm sorry about that little scene, Colin. I didn't mean to bring you and your family into the middle of our problems. And I meant what I said. I can take a cab to my brother's—" Emotions she had fought since her mother had entered the room jammed her throat, closing off her words.

Colin laid his hand over hers, still clasped tightly together in her lap. "I'm going to the funeral so I might as well let you tag along."

"Why?"

"Personally I don't like to go to funerals alone. That's why."

"No, I mean, why are you going? You didn't know my brother, did you?"

"No, I didn't. I was going because of you. I didn't want you to face the funeral alone."

The kindness in his voice touched her. She tried to picture him in her mind, but all she could see was a vague figure that was tall and muscular. She wanted to know more. As a photographer, visualizing a person had always been so important to her. "What color hair do you have?"

"Black."

"Eyes?"

"Gray."

"Is your hair long?"

"No, short and straight."

"Are you nice looking?"

Colin chuckled. "Why are you asking all these questions?"

"I'm trying to see you in my mind. I don't want you to be faceless." All her life she had worked in a world that revolved around the visual aspects of life. She saw things in her mind as though they were a still photo or a moving picture. Not being able to do that with Colin bothered her.

"I'm just an average Joe. Nothing special about me. Sorry I can't be of more use."

For a few seconds she thought of asking him to let her touch his face and try to discern his features through her fingertips. But that seemed too intimate a gesture to her, and she wasn't even sure if she could tell anything by doing it. So for the time being she would have to be satisfied with a faceless man with short black hair and gray eyes.

The overcast day reflected the mood of the crowd attending Derek St. James's funeral at Central City Cemetery. The new leaves on the trees flapped in the brisk, cool wind while the scent of freshly mowed grass laced the air. Colin walked around his SUV and opened the passenger's door to assist Emma from his vehicle.

Her drawn, pinched features held an ashen cast to them. Before leaving the confines of his car, she donned a pair of sunglasses even though the sun was hidden by a thick layer of roiling gray clouds. She clasped his upper arm and walked close to him toward the people crowded around the grave site.

"We have about twenty feet to go. There's a curb in front of you." Colin slowed as she stepped up.

Emma came to a stop. "Describe what you see. Do you know anyone in attendance? Any press?"

"No, I think your father has effectively taken care of any photographers or reporters. There is a large tent with several rows of chairs for their guests. Your mother is standing on one side of the casket and your father is on the other. Each of them has an entourage around them. I see J.T. is here with Madison Spencer, the detective from the state police."

Emma leaned close and whispered, "Checking to see

if anyone looks suspicious, no doubt. Do you really think the murderers would be here?"

Colin stared at J.T. and Madison, both scanning the faces of the people in the crowd. "They're certainly watching everyone. Hey, you said *murderers*. How do you know there was more than one? Did the sheriff say anything to you?"

She shook her head slowly, swinging around to face him. "No, but I know there was more than one person." Her brow scrunched up. "I don't know how. I just do." She stared off into space a long moment, then added, "But there's nothing else. Was there more than one person?"

"J.T. thinks there may have been, judging from the footprints at the side of the road where the shot that hit you came from. I suppose some of the footprints could have nothing to do with the person who shot you."

"Maybe." Again her eyebrows slashed down as she became lost in thought. "No, definitely there was more than one person involved."

Colin patted her hand, which was clutching his arm. "Good. That's a start. Your memory will come back."

"You know, Reverend, there is a part of me that doesn't want to remember."

"I know. You'll heal in God's time."

His reference to the Lord reminded her of what Colin did for a living. They were so different. She needed him for the time being, but she had every intention of taking back her life, and God had nothing to do with it.

Colin tensed.

"What's wrong?"

"Both of your parents are heading toward you."

FIVE

"Are my parents together?" Emma asked, straightening beside Colin, not far from Derek's grave site.

"No, they're doing their best to ignore each other."

No matter how much oxygen she drew into her lungs, there wasn't enough to calm the racing of her heart. She tightened her clammy grip on Colin's arm, glad that she wore sunglasses to conceal her eyes. When her mother chose to look beyond herself, she was uncanny at zeroing in on others' emotions and playing on them. She didn't want her mother to expose her any more than she already was.

"Darling, I was getting so worried about you."

Her mother pulled her into a hug, kissing her on both cheeks. Then her father practically wrestled her away from Marlena and embraced her awkwardly, which came as no surprise since Emma could count on one hand how many times her father had done so in the past. If Derek hadn't been William St. James's son, she could see him behind her brother's murder, especially since Derek had walked away last year from working for their father. William St. James didn't like being crossed—ever. Was that why she had blocked everything about that day at the cabin from her mind? The thought her father could be behind Derek's murder chilled her heart. Surely his ruthlessness didn't go that far?

Emma shoved away, bringing herself up against Colin, who steadied her. "I would have to be in a coma not to come to Derek's funeral. Now if you two would excuse me…" She started past her parents, hoping Colin followed because she didn't know where to go.

Her father grabbed her arm and halted her escape. "You may not like what has happened in the past between us, but I expect you to act civil in front of all our family and friends."

Do I make myself clear? was the unstated question. Although Emma couldn't see his hand, she peered in the direction of his grip on her arm. "I'm quite good at not airing our dirty laundry in public. Have I ever said anything about—" Suddenly she remembered that Colin was beside her and that he wasn't a member of the family. She snatched back the last of her sentence and pulled her arm from her father's grasp. "I'll be the dutiful daughter for all the world to see. Don't worry. Your reputation won't be tarnished by me."

"Good. Then allow me."

Her father took her hand and placed it on his arm to guide her toward the grave site. Her mother took up her position next to her on the other side. The sudden separation from Colin left Emma shivering.

"Colin?"

From behind her he said, "I'm right here."

The unspoken message in his words comforted her. He wouldn't let her father intimidate him into leaving her alone with them. In the darkness that surrounded her, he was her light. For some reason she felt a ray of hope, as though the sun had burst through the clouds to warm her chilled body.

Her father sat her between him and her mother in the front row under the tent at the grave site. The scent of flowers—she couldn't tell what kind—sweetened the air. Murmurs around her spoke of the large crowd and one woman sobbing nearby caused her to turn toward the sound. She wondered who it was but refused to ask either of her parents to be her eyes.

The somber service ticked by slowly. Each word said confirmed in Emma's mind that it hadn't been a nightmare she would awaken from soon. Her brother was dead—murdered by people who could possibly be after her, too.

At the end of the service, Colin, who sat behind her, placed his hand on her shoulder. That she knew it was him surprised her, but he didn't have to say a word. His touch had become familiar over the past few days, as though what had happened on the highway had formed a connection between them that strengthened each day.

When the guests began to file past her and her parents, the woman who was still crying, softer now, paused and took her hand within hers.

"I feel like I know you, Emma. I'm Alicia Harris. Derek and—" Tears took over and the woman released her grasp.

"Alicia? I know you and Derek were dating."

Between the sobs the woman murmured, "Over three months."

Emma reached for the woman, wanting to comfort another who had been special to her brother. Derek had talked lately about Alicia and how he had thought she might be the one. Emma's hand clasped empty air for a few seconds until Colin guided her arm in the right direction.

Squeezing Alicia's hand, Emma rose and drew her into her embrace. "I'm so sorry. I know Derek thought a lot of you."

Alicia pulled back, sniffling. "I—I—loved him. We had...talked of getting married."

Married? That took Emma by surprise. Yes, her brother had talked about Alicia, but Derek would never rush into marriage because of their parents' lousy one. "I didn't realize."

"I don't know how someone could have kill— Oh, dear, I'm sorry. I shouldn't have said anything. You were almost killed, too. Hopefully you'll be able to help the police catch the person who—" Alicia choked on the last of her sentence and began to sob again.

Unknowingly, Alicia's words sliced deeply into an unhealed wound. Emma struggled to keep her composure. Her mother put an arm around Emma as though protecting her from the woman. "Thank you for coming," Marlena said in a formal, stilted voice that conveyed her displeasure at the scene Alicia Harris was causing.

Emma sank down onto the chair, her hands quivering at the coldness her mother displayed toward someone her brother had been very interested in. But then, her mother always wanted to be center stage.

"I'm so sorry, Emma." Brandon McDonel took her hand within his and leaned down to kiss her cheek, the brush of his lips lingering a second longer than casual. "I can't believe he's gone. We'd planned to meet in Chicago at the end of the month."

Her eyes closed at the sound of Brandon's thick

voice, his emotions barely controlled. She had dated him for nearly half a year and at one time thought they might marry. Then six months ago he had backed off, immersing himself in his work at the bank, wrapped up in his climb to the top. Coming from a poor background, Brandon valued the prestigious bank he worked for.

Her throat constricted with her own feelings so near the surface. Slipping her hand from his, she dropped her head for a moment, trying to compose herself. "I appreciate you being here with me," she finally managed to say, lifting her chin.

He must have knelt in front of her, because suddenly she felt as though he was on the same level as her. He bent close. "Emma, if you need anything, please call. I know things have been strained lately, but I haven't forgotten how close we were once. I'm here for you if you want to talk about Derek or anything that happened. It must have been horrible. I want to help."

His breath fanned her cheek, his whispered words full of promise and support. Six months ago she would have clung to them. Today, they left her empty. He had been her brother's roommate in college and friend for years, but there was something missing—something she couldn't put her finger on. "I appreciate the concern."

He rose. "When are you coming home?"

"To New York?" she asked, beginning to wonder where her home really was anymore.

"Yes."

"I don't know."

"It's good to see you again, Brandon," Marlena said, drawing him away.

For once Emma appreciated her mother's interference. She ushered the people through the line quickly. Exhausted, Emma wanted to escape before she heard another "I'm sorry for your loss."

By the time Marcus Peterson closed his hands around hers, she could barely lift her arm. She needed to leave.

"Emma, Derek was not only my business partner, but a good friend. I'll miss him. If you need anything, let me know."

She murmured her thanks to Marcus, relieved that her mother took over again. Emma turned her head toward where she hoped Colin still sat. He settled his hand on her uninjured shoulder and leaned close, his male fragrance engulfing her.

"I need to go."

He helped her rise. "I'll come around and we can leave."

She blew a breath out between pursed lips. "Good."

Half a minute later, Colin reached Emma's side. She shifted so she could slip her arm through his.

"You're leaving?" Marlena asked, a frown in her voice.

"I just got out of the hospital yesterday. I'm exhausted."

"But all these people expect—"

Being careful to protect her bandaged shoulder, Emma hugged her mother loosely and kissed her on the cheek. "I'm sure they'll understand." Her nerves screamed for escape. Her heart beat slowly and painfully. Her limbs ached with every movement, the cuts on the bottom of her foot throbbing from being on her feet so much.

"Fine. Then I guess this is goodbye." Her mother pulled away and started talking to another.

Used to Marlena's dismissal if something didn't go her way, Emma turned toward her father to tell him she was going. But his loud voice whisked her words from her mind.

"I can't believe you showed up. You have some nerve, Lunsford."

"I had to see your pain for myself."

Emma gasped.

Colin tightened his arm about her as Emma's father and another man squared off.

"Get out before I have security throw you out." William St. James's face reddened, his hands fisted at his sides. He took a step toward Lunsford, a tall, thin man with a black beard.

Lunsford smiled, his teeth showing, bowed his head and disappeared into the crowd. Emma's father started after Lunsford. Someone on his other side, a petite woman, put a hand on his arm to stop him. He glared at her for a few seconds before he managed to veil his anger behind a polite facade.

"Get me out of here," Emma whispered, her face pale.

Colin didn't need further motivation to leave. He threaded his way through the mourners, all murmuring to one another about the little scene a few moments ago. At his SUV, he opened the door and helped Emma inside. She collapsed back against the seat, her arms limp at her sides, her head lolling on the headrest.

When he slipped behind the steering wheel, she turned toward him and said, "I'm sorry about that."

"Who is Lunsford?"

"One of my brother's victims."

He started the engine, almost as tired as Emma after the emotional intensity of the past hour. "Victims?"

"My brother used to work for my father doing his

dirty work. He would buy up companies in trouble. The takeover of Lunsford's company was ugly. It left the man bitter and with little in the bank when all was said and done. I think that last takeover was the reason Derek finally had to walk away from the family business. His heart wasn't in ruining others' lives. My father is much better at it."

Lord, what in the world has Emma had to live through? The more I'm with her, the more I realize she desperately needs You. Guide me in the right way to teach her the Word. There is so much more to life than what she's used to.

Emma's hand shook as she handed Colin the key to Derek's apartment. A tight band about her chest made breathing difficult. The last time she had visited she had celebrated her brother's freedom from their father a year ago. She'd helped him move from Chicago, their father's town, to Central City, where the family had originally lived years ago, before Marlena got her big break in a blockbuster movie. Now she wished she'd seen him more in the past year, the only other time being six months ago when he'd come to New York for a few days and stayed with her.

Stepping inside, she thought of the floor-to-ceiling windows overlooking the river. The view was beautiful, a beauty she wouldn't be able to see ever again. The realization she would never return to her brother's apartment nor possibly ever see *anything* struck her speechless as she grappled with her careening emotions.

Tears threatened. She swallowed the knot in her throat, but it immediately returned. Although tired and still in pain, a restlessness compelled her to come here a day after Derek's funeral for what purpose she didn't know. What did she think she would find here? Derek's murderer hiding under the bed?

"You don't have to do this today."

Colin's deep, gentle voice pulled her from her thoughts. "I know. His things need to be boxed up. I've got to start sometime now that the police have turned it over to the family." And maybe in all his belongings she could discover a hint of who had wanted her brother dead.

"The first thing I want to get is his laptop, then put all his papers from his desk in a box. He often worked from home because his company's office was in Chicago."

"Are you looking for anything in particular?"

"Yes, a piece of paper telling me who killed Derek. It wasn't random. They planned to kill him."

"How do you know? J.T. hasn't ruled out robbery. The cabin was trashed."

As so often in the past week, she reached deep into her mind for answers, but none surfaced. "I guess you could say it's my intuition."

"Let me get the boxes we brought, then we can start."

While Colin went back into the hallway where he'd left the flattened boxes he'd bought at the supercenter, Emma stood in the middle of what was her brother's spacious living room, trying to remember its layout. The leather couch should only be a few feet to the right. She groped forward and stumbled into a low table.

"Ouch!" Her legs must be black and blue from her attempts at independence the past few days. If her blindness lasted much longer, she would have to get a cane and have mobility training.

"Emma, wait. I'll help you," Colin said as he walked back into the apartment.

Frustration and anger welled up. She didn't want to have to wait for someone to escort her. She pressed the heels of her hands into her eyes, willing herself to see. "I should be able to see! What's wrong with me?"

Colin took her hands. "It'll happen when you're ready."

"I'm ready. I want to know who killed my brother, *now*. I want to help the police." The tears returned to clog her throat.

"You can't force it."

She felt the wet tracks of her sorrow running down her cheeks. She was tired of holding them inside when others were around. Colin drew her against him, and she clung to him while the sobs flowed unchecked, dampening his shirt. Slowly she became aware of her surroundings—the slightly rough texture of his shirt, his hand rubbing up and down her back, his clean, fresh scent that fit him so well, the thudding of his heart. She pulled away, wiping at her cheeks to erase all evidence of her moment of weakness. This wouldn't solve her brother's murder.

"Derek's desk should be in the first room to the right. He uses—I mean, used it for his office, or at least he did when I was here."

"We can do this another day."

"No! I have to do something productive. I feel so useless."

"Up until a few days ago you were in the hospital."

She held out her hand to him. "Please. I can't do this without you." Having to admit that out loud surprisingly didn't bother her as much as she would have thought.

Colin took her hand and led her to the room. She sat at the desk, counting the drawers, then feeling its top until she encountered her brother's laptop, running her finger around its circumference.

"We can go through this when we get back to your aunt's. But to tell you the truth, I don't know how much Derek would have put on the computer. He didn't trust them for the really important things. He certainly wasn't—" Talking and thinking about her brother brought the tears close to the surface again. She gulped and continued. "He wasn't a techie geek. I used to kid him about—" Her hand slid off the computer, her fingernails digging into her palm. The ache in her heart made it difficult to continue.

"I'll put the computer in the box."

His fingers brushed against her fist as he reached for the laptop. For a second all she wanted to do was grasp his hand and draw strength from him. She was scared. So much was happening to her, and she didn't know how to deal with it. She slipped her hands into her lap and entwined her fingers. Except for Derek, she'd always felt alone in this world, apart from everyone else. She wished she had Colin's faith.

"What's next?"

"Let's empty the drawers and sort the papers out later. Then I'd like to go through the apartment and put anything in the boxes that might give me a clue as to who would kill Derek."

"Emma, don't you think we should leave this to the police if they decide it's more than a robbery attempt?"

We? For a brief moment she didn't feel so alone. She sensed him staring at her, waiting for an answer. "It was. And I'm going to prove it. I know my brother better than anyone. We may not have seen each other a lot in the past year, but we kept in contact every week. The police might overlook something of importance. Believe me, I won't act on anything I discover. I'll turn it over to the police." She twisted about to face him next to her. "But I have to do *something*. I owe it to Derek."

The intensity in Emma's expression underscored her determination to find her brother's murderer. Colin could understand the need. The alternative would be having to deal with what was going on with her. Facing possible blindness, especially for a woman who lived by her sight, wouldn't be easy. "Then I'll help in any way I can. I'll be your eyes." He pulled up a chair to sit beside her.

"Thank you. I don't think I could have asked anyone else and, frankly, that surprises me. You're practically a stranger and yet it seems so right."

Her voice was low, almost as though she was thinking aloud, not aware that he was next to her. She felt the connection he did. Colin opened the drawer closest to him. "Do you want just the papers?"

"Take Derek's address book, and anything you feel might help. I trust your judgment."

Her belief in him pleased him, prompting him to grin. He delved into his task with enthusiasm, finishing the first drawer quickly and moving on to the next one while Emma felt around the long skinny drawer in front of her which held mostly pens, paper clips and other office supplies.

When he came to the third one, he found a thick manila folder. "This might be interesting."

"What is it?" Emma straightened and leaned toward him.

"Newspaper clippings."

"Any particular subject?"

"There's one here about Alexander Sims. There's another one about a suicide attempt by Marcella Lunsford. An old article concerning a car wreck and another detailing a house fire that happened fifteen years ago. A couple about your father and some concerning your mother. There's even a few with your name in them. Here's one with a picture of you and Brandon McDonel at a charity function. Also one about Brandon and his promotion to vice president at Premier Bank a few weeks ago."

"Why would Derek have kept newspaper articles about these people? Any with him in it?"

"The last one is an article about the new company he formed with Marcus Peterson and its enormous success. The article states that your brother could give your father a run for his money."

"I remember that one. Derek laughed about it over the phone to me. He said he was going to send Dad a copy personally. Definitely put those in the box. My brother never did anything without a good reason."

Colin had started to close the folder when his attention fell again on the top article about Alexander Sims. In the margin someone had written Alicia followed by a question mark. "Does an Alicia have a connection to Alexander Sims?"

"Why would you say that? The only Alicia I know is the woman at the funeral who was dating Derek."

Colin read the article to her, which concerned the

man's new company since he had been bought out by S&J Corporation two years ago. "Did your brother have anything to do with the acquisition of Sims's company?"

"I'm sure he did, since he headed up Dad's Research and Development Department, which was really only a glorified title for acquisitions." Emma tilted her head to the side. "I don't know of a connection between Alexander Sims and Alicia. The man hated my brother and vowed to take him down one day. Actually, right after it happened, Alexander attacked Derek at a restaurant. I've never seen Derek so angry. I was with him when it happened. He even pressed charges but later dropped them."

"Then we should check this out." Colin dropped the folder into the box, thinking of the list of people that Derek had crossed through his dealings. He was beginning to get a picture of a ruthless businessman who rivaled William St. James. How aware was Emma of her brother's true nature? Did her brother really quit working for their father because he hated what he was doing to others? Or was it something else? He felt like Daniel in the lion's den. But like Daniel, his faith would see him through this.

Emma rubbed her hand along her forehead. "That last year Derek worked for Dad, he became depressed. I was really worried about him. I think he was afraid he was becoming like Dad and didn't like it. Do you think that might be one reason he kept these articles—to remind him of what he'd almost become?"

"Maybe," he murmured, not really sure of anything.

She shook her head. "I don't know what to think anymore." Collapsing back in the chair, she closed her eyes.

Exhaustion lined her face. His heart twisted at the sight. "Let's finish boxing the desk, then go get something to eat. I don't know about you, but I'm starved."

She swung her head toward him. "I'm not very hungry, but that sounds like a good idea."

He resisted the urge to touch the circles beneath her eyes. "You need to eat something. You'll need your energy. We'll have this box to go through when we get home."

"Are you and Grace ganging up on me? I woke up this morning to the wonderful smell of baking bread and frying bacon."

Her smile transformed her face, and for a moment he glimpsed the woman she had been before tragedy struck. "Guilty. She made me promise that I would take you to a nice restaurant for lunch. She insisted on no fast food."

"Your aunt is such a contradiction. She's all tough and gruff one minute and soft and mushy the next."

"That's Grace. She's an expert at shooting and at cooking. She can flip you onto your back so fast you don't know what's happening until it's too late, then turn around and smother you with hugs and kisses and feed you the best food you've ever had." Colin opened the last drawer. "I have one left to go through."

Emma continued feeling her way through the long skinny drawer. When her fingers clasped a key, she said, "Found it." She showed him. "It's the key to Derek's safety-deposit box. I'm on the account, too. Maybe there's something in it that can help us."

"We'll grab something to eat, then go to the bank."

Colin completed emptying the last drawer, then closed the large box and lifted it into his arms. "Ready?"

Rising, Emma took hold of his elbow. "I'm actually getting hungry, after all."

"Good, because I can't lie to my aunt. She'll want to know everything you had for lunch."

At the elevator, she punched the down button while he held the box cradled in his arms. When they reached the lobby, Colin signed them out at the security guard's desk. After glancing at a bank of monitors, Colin turned toward the entrance. As they left the exclusive apartment building, he nodded at another security guard on duty out front.

"This place is fortified like Fort Knox." Colin put the box in the back seat of his SUV.

"That's why Derek bought his apartment here, since he did so much business from his home." Emma slid into the front.

He drove to a restaurant only a few blocks from Derek's in Central City. After parking in the lot next to the upscale café, he guided Emma inside, glad it was late for the lunch crowd so there weren't too many people still eating. The hostess sat them at a table in a side alcove with real potted plants surrounding them.

"Have you ever eaten here?" Emma asked, smoothing her linen napkin in her lap.

"First time. Grace suggested this restaurant. She said the salads and sandwiches were good. What are you in the mood for?"

"If they have a club sandwich, I'll take one. That should be easy enough for me to eat."

After the waitress took their order and brought them their iced teas, Emma felt along her plate until she touched her glass then lifted it to take a sip. "I've taken so much for granted in my life. I almost asked you to order at a drive-through so we could eat at the apartment."

Colin started to help her as she put her glass on the table and nearly spilled it when she set it on the end of her knife, but he held back, letting her handle it, instinctively knowing that was important. "Why didn't you?"

"Grace. In just the two days I've gotten to know her, I've learned she would never let blindness stop her from doing something she wanted to do. I've always enjoyed eating out at restaurants so I need to get used to it. I've never had to fight for much. Everything has come easy." She shrugged. "I guess some people would think I had a charmed life."

"What do you think?"

Her laugh held no humor. "No—yes, money has never been a problem, but I have two very visible parents who enjoy fighting in public as well as private and never hesitated to bring Derek and me into the middle of their battles. Not what I would call a normal childhood. Derek was my rock and that has been taken away from me."

"Have you ever thought about letting God be your rock? The Lord can't be taken away from you no matter what, if you believe."

"I haven't seen a lot of evidence of God in life."

"He's all around us. When my wife died, God was who helped me through the rough times when I wanted to sink down into my sorrow. I couldn't. I had two daughters who needed me, but it was so tempting." He covered her hand on the table. "When I was in the Gulf War and trapped behind enemy lines, the Lord saw me through. I thought I would die in the desert, but He had other plans for me."

"What?"

"After the war, I came home and became a minister. Surrounded on all four sides by the enemy, I pledged myself to the Lord. I survived without a scratch on me and haven't regretted for one day my vow to God."

She withdrew her hand. "He wouldn't have me. I've done some things in my life I'm not proud of. Until two years ago, I had an addiction that threatened to destroy me."

SIX

Sitting in the restaurant with Colin, Emma drew back, deep in memories of the days where all she had cared about was taking her pain medication. Her life had revolved around ways to get enough of what she needed to make it through each day. She looked away from him, imagining the repulsion and disappointment on his face.

"I was a drug addict."

"What happened?" he asked in a neutral voice.

"Three years ago I liked to live hard and fast. I was in a car accident. I wrapped my car around a tree. I broke both legs, along with other injuries. I ended up becoming dependent on pain medication. If it hadn't been for Derek's interference, I might still be. I owe my brother so much. He made me go to a clinic. He was there for me every step of the way. So you see why it's so important for me to find out who murdered him." *And why I must stand on my own two feet,* she thought, never wanting to turn control of her life over to anything else.

"Yes, but Emma, God doesn't expect us to be perfect. There are countless stories in the Bible where people who had sinned many times were accepted by the Lord into His fold without question. One of Jesus' disciples was a tax collector. Matthew, who was the author of one of the gospels, was hated by his people. He took from them and gave to the Romans. He was the lowest of the low, doing his own dirty work, and yet Christ called him to His side and Matthew answered the call, becoming one of His ardent believers, spreading His word among the people."

Is that possible? Is it that simple? Open your heart and let the Lord in? She wished it were, but how could it be? She didn't know what to say to Colin, was at a loss to reply to him. The silence elongated between them with sounds of people talking and eating intruding.

"Anytime you want to talk or ask questions, I'm available," Colin finally said.

"I wouldn't know where to begin," she murmured, not uncomfortable, as she thought she would be, but curious.

"If you want, you can come with Grace to church this Sunday."

The idea of sitting in front of his congregation, friends of Colin who had, no doubt, heard about what had happened to her, helpless, blind, unable even to walk down the aisle without someone guiding her, made her hesitate. "I'll think about it."

"Ah, it looks like our lunch has arrived and I'm past being hungry."

The lightness in his voice, which held no censure, prodded her to smile and say, "I have to admit I may actually eat the whole sandwich. I guess if you wait long enough for a meal, you'll eat it. I normally eat around noon."

After the waitress placed their food in front of them,

Colin said, "The sandwich is on the right side of the plate at three o'clock and the fries on the left at nine."

Emma touched the edge of the plate nearest her, then eased her hand forward until she encountered the sandwich. Picking up half of it, she bit into it. "Mmm. Grace is right. This *is* good."

When she had managed to finish part of her meal, her hunger abated, she sipped her peach tea then wiped her mouth. "Tell me about Tiffany and Amber. I don't even know what they look like."

"Although they are twins, they don't dress alike. Even their brown hair isn't the same. Tiffany wears hers short, sometimes spiked on top, like Grace, while Amber usually has hers pulled back in a long ponytail. They're petite, like their mother, and they have gray eyes, like me."

"Grace told me they're very different."

"Two sisters couldn't be as different as they are. Tiffany is athletic. Amber comes alive in front of a computer. She's a whiz and will probably end up doing something along that line when she goes to college. Tiffany's outgoing and will try anything once, which may prematurely turn my hair gray. Amber's reserved and studious. She examines a problem from every angle while Tiffany jumps in with both feet without thinking."

"I bet that can lead to problems."

He laughed. "A few. I hope Tiffany hasn't bothered you too much."

"No. She's a delight. Talks a mile a minute."

"And Amber hasn't said two words?"

"Only if I ask her a question. But then I'm not sure she could get much in with Tiffany." Emma fumbled for a fry and popped it into her mouth. "You know, I used to be like Amber."

"You were?"

"Don't sound so surprised. Living with Marlena Howard, who demanded all the limelight, wasn't easy. I learned to live in the background, especially for years when she didn't want people to know she had a daughter as old as I was."

"How old were you?"

"It started when I was a teenager. Thankfully, she is past that and in her own way is proud of the work I do. In fact, she insists I be the only photographer to take her pictures for magazines and such."

"I don't see you as shy and reserved now."

Taking another fry, she said, "In a lot of ways I still am. That's why I became a photographer instead of working in front of the camera."

"But Tiffany says you're all over the place in magazines and the newspaper. She even showed me some Internet sites devoted to you and your work."

Heat seared her cheeks. "Please don't remind me of those. That's not of my choosing."

"Not another word, then," he said with amusement.

She washed another fry down with a sip of tea. "That's it. I'm done. Any more and I'll blow my diet."

"Diet! You can't weigh more than a hundred and ten."

"In my world appearance is everything, even though I'm only the photographer."

"Your work should be all that matters."

The sadness in his voice aroused her defenses until she thought a moment about what he had said. He was right. And in his world that was true.

"Tiffany has shown me some of your pictures. They're quite good."

Thinking about her work produced a heavy ache. What was she going to do if she didn't regain her eyesight? The question she had been avoiding for days taunted her now. Especially the past few years, her work had been her life. Before her emotions took over again and she cried in front of this man a second time in one day, she needed to change the subject. "Do you think Amber would take a look at Derek's computer?"

"Why?"

"Even though my brother wasn't into computers, there might be something on the laptop that can help us."

"I'm sure she wouldn't mind. I'll ask her when we get home."

Emma sighed. "Great. But right now I don't have any idea what to do next."

"We'll go by the bank and check his safety-deposit box, then later tonight have Amber look at the computer while we go through the papers in Derek's desk. That's a start."

The bank employee slid the signature card toward Emma. Colin took the pen and gave it to her, guiding her hand to the line she needed to sign on. He noticed the last time her brother had been to the safety-deposit box was the day he died.

With his assistance, Emma followed the woman into the vault. After the bank employee opened the box, Colin waited until she left before removing the box and taking it over to the table for Emma to look through. She sat while he flipped the lid up.

"What's in it?" Emma started to reach inside.

"Nothing. It's empty."

"Empty? That's strange. Why have a box with nothing in it?"

"Your brother was here the day he was killed. He must have taken everything out then. Do you have any idea what was in it?"

"No, but he made a big deal a year ago when I was here about adding me to the signature card. I don't understand."

Colin closed the box and put it back. "I don't, either. Let's go home and see what we can find on the laptop and in the papers."

"If there's nothing there, I think we should go back to his apartment and look around some more. We should also check the cabin when the sheriff releases it."

"It was trashed."

"I know, but I don't know what else to do. I can't sit around doing nothing. I feel like a bomb is ticking down." Emma rose, leaning into the table as though the activities of the day were finally catching up with her.

"You need to rest." Colin took her arm. "Remember, you were in the hospital three days ago and were seriously injured less than a week ago."

She allowed him to lead her from the vault, resting her head against him, which underscored how tired she must be. He helped her to his SUV, then pulled out of the parking lot. She slumped against the door, her head against the window, her eyes closed.

At a stoplight he peered at her, exhaustion evident in her features, with dark circles under her eyes. *Lord, I don't know where You're taking me but I do know she needs me. Give me the right words to say to her to ease*

*her pain and help her deal with what life has thrown at
her. And help me to show her the way to You. Amen.*

"I can't thank you enough, Amber. Are you sure you
don't mind?" Emma ran her hand along the back of the
couch until she came to the end. She stepped around to
the front and settled next to the teenager.

"I don't mind, but Miss St. James, I'm not sure what
you're looking for."

"Please, call me Emma." She heard the sound of the
laptop coming on, a finely honed tension taking hold.
She hoped there was something on Derek's computer
that would indicate who hated him enough to kill him.
"I've got to say I don't know what I'm looking for. I
guess anything unusual. Maybe we could start with the
places my brother used to visit on the Internet. What do
you think?" Twisting around to face Amber, she leaned
back against the arm of the couch. The material beneath
her fingertips felt rough, as though it was brocade.
"What color is this couch?"

"Huh?"

"I was just wondering what color this couch is." In
the past, she'd taken for granted the color of an object.

"Oh, it's gold and silver. Ugly, but don't tell Aunt
Grace that," Amber whispered close to her.

"You've got my promise."

"She doesn't have very good taste when it comes to
decorating. Tiffany has tried to help her, but Aunt Grace
wants her house *her* way and what Aunt Grace wants,
she gets. Even my sister can't change her mind."

Emma sat cross-legged on the couch, enjoying the
exchange with Amber. The few times she had been

around the teenager, Amber hadn't said much, but then Tiffany had always talked for both of them. The sound of Amber's fingers flying over the keyboard filled the den. "Where is your sister?"

"At cheerleading practice. They're getting ready for camp."

"Ah, I can picture her at a game cheering the team on."

Amber chuckled. "Yeah, she's definitely the cheerleading type. If your brother had a password, what would it be?"

"You need one?"

"Yeah."

Emma thought of Derek and some of their conversations, trying to decide what her brother would use. "Let's try his birthday. August 21, 1972."

"Nope."

Emma told her some more combinations that he might use, but none of them worked. Then she remembered a dog he'd loved when he was growing up. "Try Frisky."

"It worked!" Amber typed some more. "Now let's see what I can find out." Eagerness and enthusiasm infused her voice.

Emma knew the teenager was in her element.

"The last place he visited was an auction site for pottery and baskets."

"He liked to collect Southwest Indian art. I can't believe he was doing business online. Must be Marcus's influence. His partner was always trying to get him more involved in using the computer with their business."

"I can't believe anyone *not* using a computer. Even Tiffany and Dad do."

"You had to know my brother. He was *very* different," Emma said with a laugh, remembering the fun times she'd had with him growing up. Those memories eased some of the pain of losing him, of discovering hints of a whole other side to him.

"A different auction site." Amber typed some more. "Here, he did a Google search on someone named Alicia Harris."

Emma sat straight up. "He did? When?"

"Eight days ago."

"Can you trace where he went?"

"Yeah, give me a minute."

Footfalls approaching the den pulled Emma's attention away from the teenager. She turned toward the door and knew the second Colin appeared in the entrance. Her skin tingled, an awareness zipping through her as she imagined him finding her in the room.

"Hi, Dad." Amber continued to click away.

"How's it coming, you two?"

Emma gestured toward his daughter. "She found out that Derek did a search on Alicia recently. I wonder why."

"Was that the woman who had made such a scene crying at the funeral?"

"Yes, they had been dating for three months. He was getting serious."

"Maybe she was using his computer and checking the Internet about herself?"

"I suppose that's possible."

"I've brought you something."

"You have?" Suddenly she felt like a child on her birthday.

"I borrowed some CDs from one of my congregation for you to listen to if you want. They're the Gospels of the New Testament, the story of Jesus' life. I can get Grace's CD player and put it on your bedside table."

"Thank you," she murmured, touched by his thoughtfulness and the idea he was letting her discover God on her own, not shoving his agenda down her throat.

"I'll be back in a sec."

As Colin left the room, Amber said, "Got it."

Alert, Emma shifted toward the teenager as if she could see the computer screen. "What did my brother look at?"

"Mostly newspaper articles. Alicia Harris was into a lot of charity work."

"Yeah, Derek said something about that to me. Can you read the articles to me."

"Sure."

Amber read through three short pieces about different charity projects Alicia was involved in. While she was finishing up, Colin came into the den and sat next to his daughter.

"Find anything interesting?" he asked.

"Nothing I can tell." Emma couldn't keep the disappointment from her voice. She wanted a red neon sign pointing to the murderer. It sure would make her life easier.

"Hey, here's an obituary of Alicia's mother. From there your brother did a search on Alexander Sims."

"Alexander Sims? He hated my brother. Now we're getting somewhere." Emma tingled with excitement.

"Amber, go back to the obituary," Colin cut in. A few seconds later, he added, "Did you know that Alexander Sims was Alicia's uncle?"

"No! Derek would never have dated her if he'd known."

"Well, Sims is listed as Alicia's mother's brother in the obituary."

"Maybe Derek didn't know until two days before he died."

"But didn't Alicia talk about how they were going to get engaged at the funeral?" Colin asked.

"She did but I thought she was exaggerating."

"Maybe she was lying. Maybe Derek found out about her connection to Sims and broke it off."

Emma's excitement grew. "Why would Alicia date my brother? Her uncle thought Derek was responsible for his downfall. He even threatened publicly to ruin Derek."

"Maybe he and Alicia had come up with a plan?"

"To murder Derek?"

Colin sighed. "Probably not, but then people have murdered for less than that."

"You're right. I can't rule anyone out at this time. I'll put her down on my list."

"As well as her uncle," he added. "After we go through your brother's papers, maybe we'll have another suspect."

The way Colin said *we* so casually and naturally, as though he had been doing it for a long time, warmed Emma. She didn't feel alone—in fact she hadn't since she had come home from the hospital. "I think I should add Jerry Lunsford to the list, too, especially since he came to the funeral. He definitely held a grudge against Derek."

"I thought your father was going to get into a fight at the grave site."

At her remembrance of the scene, Emma shivered. "My father and Jerry Lunsford have a history together— not a good one. Amber, have you found anything else?" Emma asked, hearing the tap, tap of the keys as the teenager typed.

"No, nothing that means anything. He visited a site for fishermen. That's about all."

"Derek was looking forward to spending a few days on the lake. He wanted to fish and hadn't in months. Even though he only lived an hour away, he rarely came to the family cabin. With the new business venture he'd been so busy. This was his first real break."

Her emotions crammed her throat as she recalled their last phone call, the night before she'd driven down. His casual comment about wishing his life had turned out differently had stunned her. She'd never sensed that feeling before with him. Weariness had been woven through every word he had spoken. He'd wanted to make sure she was coming down because he'd needed to talk to her about something. With her curiosity piqued, she'd tried to get him to talk over the phone, but he'd said they would have plenty of time the next evening, that it wasn't a big deal. Or had it been and he'd been trying to protect her for a while longer? She closed her eyes, tears pricking her lids. She'd never know what he'd wanted to tell her. She should have insisted. Maybe then she would have answers to the questions plaguing her.

Amber shut the computer. "I wish I could have found more."

Emma blinked the tears away and patted Amber's arm. "You were terrific. Thanks for helping."

"Anytime!" Amber said, sliding the computer onto Emma's lap. "I'd better get home and finish my homework, but let me know if I can help you again."

"You bet." Emma hugged the laptop to her, listening to the teenager's footsteps recede.

"Thank you."

Emma turned toward Colin. "Why?"

"The smile on my daughter's face was priceless. Amber often gets overshadowed by Tiffany."

Still clutching the laptop to her chest, Emma asked, "Does she have a computer?"

"We have one the whole family uses. It's old though by computer standards."

Emma thrust the laptop toward him. "Here, take this for Amber. Knowing my brother, I'm sure this is state-of-the-art equipment even if he didn't like using it. He always got the best."

Colin gently pushed it back. "I can't take that."

"Please. You and your family have done so much for me. Let me do this for Amber. She should have a top-notch computer to work on, especially if she's thinking of going into that area in college." She placed the laptop on the couch between them, hoping he would accept the gesture of thanks. "Besides, she can thoroughly check it out to make sure there isn't anything else on it that might help us."

His chuckle floated to her. "You're mighty persuasive, Miss St. James."

"Good. I'm glad that's settled. So, are you ready to go through the box?"

"Ready, willing and able. I think we should start with the newspaper articles. Your brother took time to cut them out for a reason."

"You know it's not that surprising when I think about it. As a kid he used to cut out every article about Dad or Mom. He kept them in a scrapbook. I guess it was a habit he didn't stop when he became an adult. Why don't you read me the article about Jerry Lunsford's wife trying to commit suicide? I hadn't realized she had. When did it happen?" she asked, rubbing her hand along her chin.

"Last month. There's a follow-up article about his wife being released from the hospital dated two weeks ago. The first one says, 'Marcella Lunsford, distraught over losing her family home to creditors, following a bitter, hostile takeover of her husband's company by S&J Corporation, decided to take her own life by jumping off Highway 98's bridge.'"

After Colin read the two articles out loud, Emma sank back against the cushion, shaking her head. "That poor woman. Now confined to a wheelchair. I can see why Jerry Lunsford came to the funeral. He's distressed over his wife and wanting to blame someone." She didn't want to think about her brother's part—albeit indirect—in Marcella's suicide attempt. Why had Derek cut out the articles? Because he felt guilty? Or was it something else? Was this incident what had prompted Derek to tell her that last evening he wished his life had been different?

"This does give Jerry Lunsford a good reason to hate your brother…enough reason to murder him."

For the hundredth time she wished she could see Colin's expression. His voice was schooled into a neutral tone, but how could he not react to what he had read and make some judgments concerning her brother? She loved Derek and she was having her doubts. "Yes, he's definitely on the list. Read me the next article." Emma sucked in a deep breath and held it for a few extra seconds to steel herself.

"This one is about Alexander Sims."

Emma heard the rustle of papers as Colin must have picked up the article. He had started to read when his cell phone chimed. He stopped and answered it.

"I'll be right there. Don't worry." After flipping the phone closed, he said, "One of my congregation was just taken to the hospital. His wife thinks he was having a heart attack and called the ambulance. I told Rene I would meet her at the hospital." He rose. "We'll have to finish this tomorrow. Okay?"

Emma pushed to her feet. "Of course." As she listened to Colin cross the den, she added, "I hope he's all right."

"So do I. He has five children."

The weary urgency in Colin's voice tugged at her heart. She wanted to accompany him if for no other reason than to comfort him while he was comforting another. Who did Colin lean on? The answer immediately came to her: God.

She stood by the couch in the den for a long time. She didn't like what she was discovering about Derek and the work he had done for their father. She really shouldn't be surprised because she knew what her father was capable of. Money and power were everything to him. Thankfully Derek had gotten out before being totally corrupted. Or had he? She wondered if she didn't know her brother as well as she thought. She made a mental note to look into the new business venture he had been a partner in.

Sounds of Grace moving around upstairs finally intruded into Emma's mind. Bone tired, she used the couch to guide her toward the hallway. Slowly, because she was still learning the layout of the downstairs, she groped her way to her bedroom, her hand trailing along the hall-way wall. At the entrance she counted the necessary steps to the bed and sank down on it. The exhaustion she had tired to ignore for the past few hours finally washed over her, and she collapsed back on the cover, rolling over onto her side, her head cushioned on a pillow.

She should get ready for bed. But the very thought was too much as her eyelids closed and sleep de-scended quickly....

Pitch blackness surrounded her. Out of the darkness a vague faceless man floated past, then another. Suddenly she saw her brother in a chair, tied to it, his features contorted into a mask of pain. Blood poured from his mouth. People stood around him—Alexander Sims, Jerry Lunsford, Alicia Harris, her father, her mother—all laughing at Derek. He screamed over and over, the sound deafening.

Emma shot up in bed, blackness surrounding her. Her heart hammered against her rib cage. Her rapid breathing disturbed the quiet. Beads of sweat streamed down her face.

She brought her legs up and hugged them to her chest, laying her head on her knees. Her heart still beat so hard it roared in her ears.

She was tired, but she didn't want to sleep—or dream. With shaky hands she scooted herself to the side of the bed, trying to decide what to do to keep herself from falling back to sleep. Then she remembered the CDs Colin had brought her. She felt the wooden surface of the night table until she touched the CD player. When she punched the first button, a deep masculine voice filled the air with the Gospel According to Matthew. She smiled at the choice Colin had made for her and leaned back against the headboard.

Riveted to the words, she listened until she could no longer keep her eyes open. Closing them, she curled up on the pillow and continued to listen to the Gospel until weariness whisked her away into a dreamless world.

"What do you mean you haven't searched Derek's apartment?"

Roy gripped the phone so tightly his hand hurt. "I tried to get past the security guards. I couldn't."

"Then try harder. I need that evidence now. If it wasn't at his cabin, it has to be in his apartment. You'd better find it before someone else does. I already know that Emma paid a visit to Derek's bank. Obviously it wasn't in there, and they didn't find it at the apartment yet."

Or *he* would have been arrested, Roy thought. "Boss, I'll study the security layout and come up with a plan. We're still keeping an eye on the woman. If you change your mind and want us to take her out, let me know."

The click on the phone told Roy the extent of his employer's displeasure. Silence mocked him. He'd better find a way into Derek St. James's apartment and fast. No one crossed his employer and lived for long—he knew that from the past.

SEVEN

Emma sipped the coffee, listening to Grace move about the kitchen. "Colin didn't tell you where he was taking me?"

"No. Just to dress very casually."

Even the act of dressing required some assistance in order to make sure she didn't wear mismatched articles of clothing. Thankfully Grace had helped her label her clothes so she could now dress by herself.

The ringing of the phone cut into the silence. Grace picked it up and said, "Hello?" A few seconds later she placed the receiver in its cradle, muttering, "Another hang up. I don't like it."

"Blocked number?"

"Yeah. This makes the fifth one in two days."

"Someone's keeping tabs on us."

"I think you're right."

Grace's footfalls came toward the kitchen table and the scrape of the chair across the tile sounded in the air. "I talked to J.T. about putting a trace on my phone, but he didn't think it would do any good since the person only stays on a few seconds. He's having a patrol drive by every hour, though."

"And I have my very own bodyguard." Emma took another drink of her coffee, feeling surprisingly safe with Grace in the house.

"Still, I want to teach you some more defensive moves. How about when you get back later this afternoon?"

"Yes." Resting her elbow on the table, Emma put her chin in her palm. "I wouldn't want to meet you in a dark alley or, for that matter, in a lit one."

"I grew up in the deep South and was brought up to be genteel. My mother was shocked when I announced I wanted to go into the army. She still can't believe I can throw a man bigger than me and can shoot a person between the eyes."

Grace's thick drawl belied the image her words produced in Emma's mind. A knock at the back door followed by a key being inserted into the lock alerted Emma that Colin had arrived.

Colin entered the kitchen. "Hello, ladies. Are you ready to go, Emma?"

She rose. "Only if you tell me where we're going."

After a few seconds Colin said, "To the cabin."

Emma's breath caught in her throat. "I see. When were you going to tell me?"

Another few seconds of silence. "On the way. I didn't want you thinking too much about it."

"So you were going to spring it on me?"

"Yup."

"Chicken."

"No, just not wanting to cause you any more undue stress."

She leaned into the table, her fists perched on its top. "I've got news for you. I *want* to go to the cabin. Maybe revisiting the scene—" a lump rose in her throat, but she swallowed and continued "—will help me remember what happened. I need to remember, if we're going to catch the people responsible for my brother's murder. You don't have to protect me. I'm stronger than you think." If she said it enough, maybe it would be true.

"Sorry. I apologize for misjudging you. Ready?"

Emma came around the table, running her hand along its surface. When Colin nudged her with his arm, she took it and said, "See you later, Grace. I look forward to the lesson this afternoon."

On the drive to the cabin, Emma asked, "What happened at the hospital? Is your parishioner all right?"

"Thank the Lord it wasn't a heart attack. Just a bad case of indigestion. He's resting comfortably at home. I went by this morning before picking you up."

"Oh, good. Will you be able to come over this evening and help me go through the rest of Derek's papers?"

"I'd planned on it. I asked J.T. to stop by later so he could hear some of our theories. Is that all right?"

"Sure. Maybe he'll have some news."

"I'm having him check on any strangers in the area. Since Crystal Springs is relatively small, strangers usually stand out. Except this is a good fishing season, so there are more people than usual staying out at the lake."

"Have the press finally left?" she asked, thinking about the few who had tried to interview her at Grace's house and hadn't gotten anywhere with Colin's aunt guarding her privacy.

"I think J.T. said one or two are still around, but with your parents' departure most have left. All right, we're here." Colin turned onto the road that led to the cabin.

Her heart began to pound and a thin layer of perspiration coated her upper lip and forehead. She could do this. She had to. If he hadn't brought her today, she would have asked him to. She desperately hoped this visit would spark a memory—anything.

To take her mind off the approach to the cabin, Emma said, "Grace has asked me to go with her to church, too."

"Will you?"

"Maybe," she said, not quite sure she should commit.

He stopped his SUV and turned off the engine. "Are you ready for this?"

"As ready as I'm going to be." She heaved a deep sigh and pushed open the door.

As she climbed out of the car, Colin rounded it and came to her side. "You call the shots."

"Don't use that word around me," she said with a laugh.

"Sorry. The cabin is about four yards directly in front of you."

She moved a few feet from the SUV. The warmth of the sun caressed her face while a gentle breeze played with her hair, a hint of honeysuckle carried with it. A rivulet of sweat rolled down her face.

I can do this.

She remembered the parable of the lost sheep she'd heard the night before on the CD. *He rejoices more over that sheep than the ninety-nine that did not go astray.* Was that true? Was God with her, a lost sheep, if only she asked?

With the words of the Gospel According to Matthew running through her mind, she approached the cabin, Colin next to her, guiding her. When he indicated, she mounted the steps to the porch, her heart beating so fast her breathing became shallow.

She stopped. "Where is the window?"

"Two feet to the left."

She cautiously walked toward it with her arm outstretched. When she felt the pane, she froze. Chilled even though the temperature was warm, Emma shuddered. She knew something had happened at this window. She forced herself to press close to it, her trembling hands flattened on the glass.

In her mind, a figure emerged, just out of focus in the distance. Tall. Thin. Something familiar niggled at her. Was this the man who had shot her brother? Was this the man who had beaten him?

Startled by her last silent question, she asked, "Was Derek beaten up before he was shot?"

"Yes. Do you remember something?"

"Yes." She squinted as though that would help her to see the person in her mind, but his features didn't come into view. "No, not really. At least, I'm not sure if what I'm remembering is real or not."

"What is it?"

"A tall, thin man, perhaps six feet." Throwing all her concentration into the task, she strained, trying to make out some feature that would tell her who the man was. "There's something familiar about him, but I don't know what it is." Her voice rose with her churning frustration. The hands flat on the pane balled into fists, and she had to refrain herself from pounding against the glass. "Why can't I remember? I *need* to."

Colin's hand on her shoulder kneaded the tensed

muscles bunched around her neck. "You will when you can handle it."

"I can now."

"Are you so sure about that? You probably saw your beloved brother murdered before your eyes. That isn't something you'll ever be able to dismiss when you do finally remember—and I feel you will, one day. You're already remembering bits and pieces. It'll fall into place."

The feel of his gentle hands massaging her tension tempted her to lean back against him and draw comfort from his embrace. He had given her so much, and she knew his reason was tied up in the guilt he felt at having hit her with his SUV. "I want you to know I don't blame you for what happened on the highway. Your presence saved my life."

The rubbing motion of his fingers stilled. Tension whipped down his length, transmitted to her through his touch. "I don't think I'll ever forget the accident. I thought I'd killed you."

She twisted around. She found his face and cupped her hands on either side, feeling the smooth skin of his jaw. "You listen to me. I was shot first. If you hadn't been there, they would have finished me off. I owe you my life. And I just realized I haven't thanked you, Colin Fitzpatrick. You're a good man."

Silence reigned for a long minute before he leaned toward her, his breath fanning her cheek. Her hands slipped to his shoulders.

"I'm going to kiss you," he murmured right before his lips grazed hers ever so softly, giving her a chance to pull away if she wanted.

She didn't want to. She welcomed the caress of his

mouth as he deepened the kiss, and for a brief moment in time she forgot where she was. Her senses honed in on the feel of Colin's lips against hers, of his masculine scent teasing her nostrils, of the slightly rough texture of his hands now cradling her face, their warmth searing the edges of her frozen heart with his tenderness.

When he pulled back, he whispered in a raspy voice, "I shouldn't have done that, but I've wanted to for days. You're a remarkable woman."

"You're going to make me blush and I don't blush." Colin was causing feelings inside of her that she had never experienced before, and that frightened her. They didn't live in the same world. One day she would have to go back to hers, resume her old life. And she didn't want to hurt this man or be hurt by him.

"Are you ready to go inside?" he finally asked, his voice more in control now.

"Yes. You can describe to me what you see. I don't know what good it'll do, but maybe something will click."

When he opened the door to the cabin, the one over-riding smell that assaulted her was a cleaning product masked with a scent of pine. She hadn't expected that, had even steeled herself for the metallic odor of blood. "Did someone clean up in here?"

"I asked J.T. to remove any evidence that…"

His voice faded into the eerie silence as though the world had come to a standstill with her perched on the threshold into the cabin. She tried to form words to finish his sentence. He was trying to protect her again. "Where Derek was murdered?"

"Yes."

There was a world of emotion in the answer he

gave her, as though he had known her brother and cared as much as she did. He touched her deep in her heart, where she hadn't thought it was possible. Breathing became difficult, her lungs feeling compressed, aching. She turned away from the room, staring out the open door, desperate to inhale fresh air, not laced with a cleaning product used to cover the stench of death.

"We don't have to do this today if you want to leave."

Again his hand settled on her shoulder, gently conveying his continuous support. She covered it, squeezing it. "Yes, I do. There may be answers here somewhere and I can't *not* do it." She spun around, straightened herself and said, "Describe the room."

Colin stood next to her, his arm plastered against hers. "The place has totally been trashed and the sheriff hasn't touched any of that. Every drawer has been pulled out and the contents dumped onto the carpet. The couch and chairs have been slashed and even the stuffing yanked out. Pictures on the wall were removed and the backs torn off. Even the kitchen table was overturned."

"They were looking for something. But what?"

"Did Derek say anything to you that last time he called you? Was anyone threatening him recently?"

"Besides the couple of threats he had received when working for my father?"

"Yeah."

"No, but he had insisted I come to the cabin now. I wanted to wait until next month when I had more time. I had to clear my calendar in order to get away longer than a few days, but Derek wouldn't take no for an answer and I couldn't tell him no. Not after all he had done for me. I needed the break and we hadn't seen each other much this past year with him starting his new business."

"Did it sound like something was troubling him?"

Emma closed her eyes as though that would help her think better. "Yes—" she tilted her head "—his voice held an urgency to it. I wondered about it at the time then dismissed it as stress. He wanted to tell me something, but I never thought it could lead to something like this." She gestured toward the messy cabin.

"There are two doors that open into this large room."

"One's the bedroom and the other's a bathroom."

"Let me check them out. It's hard to move around in here without tripping over something."

Colin left her side, and she listened to the muffled sound of his footsteps crossing the carpeted floor, the creak of the door as he investigated one of the rooms. Her brother had tried to modernize the cabin and make it more livable with indoor/outdoor carpet, new appliances in the kitchen, better plumbing and furniture. And she could see none of those touches he had been excited about.

The hairs on the nape of her neck tingled, and for just a few seconds she felt as though she had a big red bull's-eye on her back. She carefully stepped away from the entrance into the cabin, her foot pushing some books out of the way so she could stand against the wall next to the door. But still, the feeling she was being watched encased her in a cold sweat. Her heartbeat crashed against her chest at an alarming rate.

"Is it any different than in here?" she called, needing to hear her voice in the sudden quiet. Her dark world pressed in on her.

"No, everything that can be has been destroyed, slashed or ripped apart."

"So if there was something in here they wanted, they got it."

"I would say yes." Colin strode back toward her. The nearer he came, the calmer her heart beat.

"Then, we might never know who's behind Derek's murder."

"There's still you."

Emma sank back against the wall, letting it support most of her weight. She ground her palms into her eyes, willing herself to see, to remember.

Colin clasped her wrists and pulled her hands away from her face. "Don't force it, Emma. It'll happen."

"You don't know that." Anger swelled into her chest, stiffening her body.

She jerked from his hold and twisted away, stepping out onto the porch, gulping in deep breaths of the fresh, moisture-laden air. With her shoulders hunched, she stared down, a black void the only thing she saw. "I want this to end, *now*."

Colin approached her from behind. "I don't think there's anything else we can accomplish here. Let's leave. It looks like it might rain soon."

As Emma walked with Colin to his SUV, the wind picked up. In the distance she heard thunder rumble. The feeling she was being watched still clung to her, and she paused at the door to ask in a whisper, "Do you see anyone in the woods?"

"Get in." Colin's voice roughened even though his hand on her arm was gentle as he assisted her into his vehicle.

A minute later he opened the driver's door and

climbed in. "I didn't see anyone, but the trees are thick and could easily hide someone. Why did you ask?"

"Just a feeling I've had since being in the cabin. Probably nerves."

"Maybe." He backed up his SUV, then drove forward, turning toward the highway. "But I've always respected a person's gut feeling."

She shivered. "Then you think there was someone back at the cabin watching?"

"The people who killed Derek are still out there, and you're the only one who might know something. We'll have to be more careful in the future. I didn't think anyone was following us, but you better believe next time I'll know for sure."

"Maybe they didn't find what they were looking for, and since the sheriff is finished with the cabin, they came back to look some more."

"That's a possibility. If there was something valuable that someone wanted, where would Derek hide it?"

"I would have said the safety-deposit box, but we know that's empty. Maybe his apartment? The security there is tight."

"Tomorrow, after church, let's go back to Central City and check his apartment again. We didn't really look around much beyond his desk." He made a turn onto the highway.

"I've decided to go with Grace to church. I know how much it means to her and I wouldn't want her to feel she had to stay home because I needed someone to watch me."

"Is that the only reason?"

"What other reason would there be?" She didn't want to tell him she was curious about God, that she had spent hours the night before listening to the New Testament CDs he'd lent her. Her feelings concerning faith in the Lord were too tender and raw to expose them to anyone else—even Colin.

"I'm still puzzled why Derek has these articles concerning a hit-and-run and a house fire. How did he know the Johnsons, who owned the house that burned down, or Clay Mitchell, who was hit by the car?" Emma scrubbed her hands down her face, her brain overloaded from all the information Colin had read in the past hour.

"Do you think either one was involved in a company he took over?"

"Maybe. That would make sense. He has articles concerning Alexander Sims and Jerry Lunsford, and I know they were involved in companies my brother took over." She shifted on the couch in the den, her shoulder where the bullet had passed through aching more than usual from all her activity of late.

"Is there any way we can find out?"

Every time he said *we,* her heart melted a little more. His family had made her feel so much a part of them. She'd never really had that. Even though she and her brother had been close as adults, while growing up they'd lived in two different households after their parents had divorced and hadn't seen each other much until they had graduated from high school. "Probably the quickest way would be for me to call my father and ask him."

"He'd know?"

"My dad would know every company his corporation took over and whose lives he messed up. He derived great pleasure from controlling others and was so angry at Derek when he left."

"Can you make that call?" Colin asked as the front doorbell rang.

The question hung in the air between them as they listened to Grace answering the door. Emma wasn't sure she could call her father. Her stomach clenched every time she thought of the brief encounters with her father after the accident and at the funeral.

"I will if I have to, but let's check out these articles further on the Internet," Emma said as footsteps approached the den. "Maybe the newspapers they were in had other stories that might help us figure out the relationships between Derek and the Johnsons and Clay Mitchell."

"What relationships?" J.T. asked, entering the den.

Emma felt Colin rise from the couch and walk toward J.T. "We're going through some newspaper articles that Derek collected and kept in his desk in his apartment. It was important to my brother, so we thought it might be important to his murderer."

Colin again sat next to her, placing something in her lap. She felt the large leather handbag and knew it was hers. "You found my purse?"

"A hiker discovered it on the side of the highway coming into town."

Emma stuck her hand inside and felt different items—her wallet, her cell phone, her makeup bag, a pen, a travel bottle of lotion.

"Everything's there—your credit card, several hundred dollars—so I can definitely rule out robbery. They wouldn't have thrown it away with everything still inside untouched."

Emma put it on the floor by her feet. "Thanks for bringing it to me."

"You're welcome. So tell me some more about these newspaper articles."

"Maybe you could do some checking about the people in these two articles." The paper rustled as Colin passed the newspaper clippings to J.T. "What do you think?"

"Let me see. Arson and a hit-and-run accident. There should be a police record. Have you two come up with anything else?"

"A short list of people who might want to see Derek St. James dead."

"Can I see it?" J.T. asked, a squishing sound indicating he sat in the leather lounge chair across from the couch.

Emma leaned back against the cushion, the throbbing in her shoulder intensifying as though reminding her of what had happened less than two weeks before. "It's not down on paper. But there's Alexander Sims and his niece, Alicia Harris, who happened to be dating my brother right before he died. Then there's Jerry Lunsford, the man who caused a scene at the funeral. For that matter, Brandon McDonel and my brother had a falling out about six months ago when Derek came to New York. Neither would discuss it."

Colin put the articles back in their folder and stacked it on top of the other papers in the box. The clippings had been the only thing of interest in Derek's desk. Everything else had been documents concerning his new company, which was doing very well. "You never said anything about Derek and Brandon fighting."

"I just thought about it. It was around the time Brandon and I decided not to get married. Maybe Derek wasn't happy with Brandon backing out of the engagement. I tried to tell Derek I was perfectly fine with the decision. I think Brandon and I were friends who decided to date so we wouldn't be so lonely."

"Have *you* come up with anyone?" Colin asked J.T., feeling more and more out of his element. He wasn't a detective, and yet something drove him to help Emma, as though they were in a race and the loser could possibly die, too.

"I've been looking into his partner. Money is often the cause of murder."

"But the partnership doesn't go to Marcus. I inherit my brother's shares of the company."

"Yeah, I know, but something doesn't add up with the company. Marcus has a few friends who are… unsavory."

Emma jerked forward. "What do you mean?"

"Madison's checking around."

"Do you think my brother was involved in something illegal?"

The astonishment in Emma's voice mirrored his own. The developing picture of her brother wasn't of a nice, kind man, but Colin hadn't thought of Derek as being crooked. In fact, her brother had seemed like a man trying to put his life in order, to make something worthwhile of it.

J.T. frowned. "I don't know. Just a few anomalies that we're checking out."

Emma sank back on the couch again, rubbing the place where a small bandage still covered her wound. Exhaustion carved deep lines into her face. This had been a long, emotion-filled day.

Colin slipped his hand over hers on the cushion. "Please keep us informed, J.T."

"Will do. Have you remembered anything else, Emma?"

"Not much. I think one of the men was about six feet tall and thin. I'm not even sure that's right."

"I'll keep that in mind." J.T. stood. "We're checking out any strangers in the area, but that description will fit a lot of men."

Colin chuckled. "Good luck. Isn't the fishing derby starting in a few days?"

"Yup, which hasn't made the task an easy one. Emma, if you remember anything at all, please call me day or night. You never know what might be important."

"I'll walk you out." Colin followed J.T. from the den.

"How's she really doing?" J.T. asked at the front door.

Colin lowered his voice, aware at how attuned Emma was becoming to sounds. "As to be expected, she's hurting and trying to deal with it, herself."

"She's lucky that she has you looking out for her. You haven't seen anything suspicious, have you?"

"You'll be the first to know. I will tell you that she felt someone was watching her today at the cabin."

"I'll have one of my deputies check it out. But it's probably nothing. I can't see the murderers returning to that cabin. They either got what they came for or there was nothing there in the first place."

"Yeah, it was a mess. I'm kind of glad Emma didn't have to see that."

J.T. opened the front door. "Take care. See you tomorrow at church."

After the sheriff left, Colin stood for a moment in his

aunt's foyer. Seeing that cabin today brought back memories of another time in his life, a time he had wanted to forget. He stared down at his hands. They shook. He could remember killing with them and the torment that had plagued him as though a piece of his soul had been ripped from him.

Lord, I can't be pulled back into the past. It nearly destroyed me once. I feel You want me to help Emma, but the price may be too high.

EIGHT

Drained both physically and emotionally, Emma laid her head on the back cushion of the couch in the den and stared up at the ceiling, not caring at the moment that all she saw was darkness. How could her brother have so many enemies? It was as though their father had infected him with his ruthlessness. For the first time she really appreciated the fact that she had been raised by her mother.

"Are you all right?" Colin asked, his deep, reassuring voice penetrating her thoughts.

Emma straightened on the couch. "I'm fi—" she stopped, deciding she couldn't pretend she was okay. "No, I'm not all right. It isn't every day a person discovers what her brother was really like."

Colin sat next to her, taking her hand within his. "No one is perfect. Your brother had his strengths and weaknesses as we all do. What you've discovered these past few days doesn't change that he loved you very much and was good to you and for you. That can't be taken away."

"But look at the lives he ruined. Jerry's wife tried to commit suicide because of Derek."

"I suspect there's more to that story. Usually one incident doesn't drive a person to suicide. There are other circumstances involved. Probably ones your brother had nothing to do with."

"Still, the glimpses I've seen of Derek don't fit my picture of him."

"And you want that picture back?"

"Yes. Desperately."

His hand about hers tightened. "Focus on Derek's good. He obviously didn't like what was happening to him or he wouldn't have quit working for your father."

"But there could be irregularities at the company he started with Marcus?"

"We don't know that for sure. And even if there are, did your brother know about them? What if his partner is crooked?"

"What if Derek found out?"

"That could be a motive for murder."

Emma trembled. Another person who could have wanted her brother dead. *The list just gets longer and I don't even know if we have everyone on it.* "What time is it? I heard Grace go upstairs a while ago."

"You did? You're getting quite good at hearing things most of us tune out. It's ten-thirty. I'd better call it a night. Got a long day tomorrow."

Emma wasn't sure she would be able to sleep, but she wouldn't keep Colin up. She rose, stretching her cramped muscles from sitting so long on the couch. "Will you walk me to my room?"

"Why, it would be my pleasure."

She settled her hand on his arm right above his elbow. "Lead the way. If I did, I'm so tired that I'd probably run us into a wall."

"How's getting around the house going?" Colin

guided her around the coffee table then toward the door that led to the hallway.

"Good thing I can't see my legs. They have to be black-and-blue. But today I only ran into one piece of furniture. Much better than yesterday."

At the door to her bedroom, Colin paused. "I like your attitude."

"I finally decided self-pity wouldn't help me. Besides, Grace wouldn't let me feel sorry for myself. She's quite a woman."

"Yeah, we're lucky to have her as part of our family."

"Thank you, Colin." She reached up to cup his cheek. "What for?"

"For being here for me." She placed her free hand along the other cheek, touching the roughened texture of a day's growth of beard.

"You're welcome."

"There's something I've been wanting to do. I want to figure out what you look like. Do you mind if I feel your face?"

"No."

His husky reply sent a shiver skittering down her spine. She ran her fingers along his strong, angular jawline, then across his forehead, smooth, crease-free. The slope of his nose indicated a well-proportioned one for his face. With fingertips tingling in anticipation, she saved his full lips, curved slightly upward, for last.

"Well, what is the verdict?"

"Pleasing. When I regain my eyesight, I would love to photograph you."

"It's a date."

The very word "date" heightened her awareness of

the man before her. She knew his distinctive fresh scent, like the woods around the cabin, the deep, rich sound of his voice with a hint of a Southern drawl, the gentle touch of his hands. But still she didn't have a visual picture of him in her mind. It had bothered her initially, but lately it hadn't been as important to her, a woman who had lived by her camera.

"Good night, Emma."

Colin brushed his lips across hers, taking possession of her mouth with a kiss that curled her toes and gave her goose bumps. When he left, quivering, she sank back against the door, listening to his footfalls as he headed for the foyer. Already she missed him.

Twisting around, she pushed open her bedroom door and entered. She was in serious trouble that had nothing to do with her brother's murder. Her heart was involved with Colin, and she was going to end up deeply hurt if she didn't stop herself from falling in love with him. Too much in her life was unsettled. Not to mention, she and Colin were from different worlds.

Making her way to her bed, she sat and turned on the CD player. She knew sleep would elude her. Her body was willing but her mind was in turmoil. She leaned back and began to listen to the words of the Gospel According to Mark.

Sitting in the front pew between Grace and Amber, Emma listened to Colin's strong voice as he gave a sermon on forgiveness, especially God's forgiveness. She had no reference point to a loving Father freely forgiving a child for a transgression. The idea that the Lord did astonished her. The last of Colin's words from 1

John stayed with her throughout the rest of the service. *If we confess our sins, He is faithful and just to forgive us our sins, and to cleanse us from all unrighteousness.*

Even a sinner like me, Lord?

Yes, the answer seeped deep into her heart.

Her breath caught. While people were singing around her, Emma stood silent, overwhelmed with a sense of peace she'd never felt in her life, safe, as if no one wanted to hurt her. As though she had finally come home.

"We congregate in the rec hall after the service for snacks and coffee." Grace sidled toward the center aisle.

"I'm not very hungry after that big breakfast you prepared. I usually never eat first thing in the morning. But I wouldn't have missed those blueberry pancakes for anything."

"Doesn't Aunt Grace make the best?"

Amber's question behind her caused Emma to turn to the teenager. "I haven't eaten anything that *wasn't* wonderful at Grace's. I could use some lessons."

Colin's aunt paused at the end of the pew. "Tomorrow I have to make some cookies for a meeting of the Sunday school teachers Monday evening. We can begin your lessons then."

"Excuse me, Grace, but that might be a little hard. I can't see."

"You can still help me. Earn your keep." Grace started forward, with Emma's hand at her elbow.

"You're a hard taskmaster," Emma said with a laugh.

"You're just finding that out?" Amber took up a position on the other side of Emma.

Flanked between Amber and Grace, Emma felt prepared to meet the other parishioners. When she entered the rec hall, the noise level inundated her. There must be a mob of people who stayed after the service for coffee and companionship. The thought made her hesitate, not sure she was ready to meet everyone. Her vulnerability at her situation resurfaced. All her insecurities leadened her steps, and she hung back.

"What's wrong, Emma?" Grace asked, pausing, too.

"There are so many people," was all she could say to explain the feelings she experienced.

"All eager to meet you and offer their condolences. They've been praying for your recovery."

"They don't know me."

"That doesn't stop them from caring and praying for you."

Emma fought to keep her mouth from falling open in surprise. She'd never had someone praying for her in her whole life. The concept was humbling. She began moving forward at Grace's side. A few seconds later, Grace introduced her to one couple, who were followed by a family of four, then another husband and wife.

When twenty minutes had passed, Emma felt loved and overwhelmed with all the names of people who cared enough to pray for her and her family. Her hand had been patted and shaken more than she could ever remember. Her arm even ached from it, but that didn't matter.

Awed emotions jammed her throat, making it impossible to say anything when Colin and Tiffany finally joined her.

"Would you like something to drink or eat?" Colin asked, taking her hand to guide her toward the refreshment table.

Emma nodded.

"Coffee?"

"Yes, please," she finally managed to say around the lump still lodged in her throat.

"A cookie?"

She shook her head.

Colin placed a mug in her hand. "Black with one scoop of sugar, just the way you like it."

She turned away, fighting the tears that now shone in her eyes. Something as simple as someone knowing how she took her coffee threatened to send her over the edge.

Colin took her arm. "Let me show you something in the kitchen."

He whisked her out of the rec hall so quickly she spilled some of her drink. "Slow down! Remember the coffee," she said as a tear slipped from her eye and rolled down her cheek.

"Oh, sorry." He plucked the mug from her hand and must have set it on a counter from the sound it made. "Are you burned?"

"I'll survive. Why are we in the kitchen?" she asked with a sniffle.

"I thought you might need some time to compose yourself."

Again Colin had demonstrated how attuned he was to her, which continued to amaze her. "Your congregation is wonderful. I feel like I've met a hundred new friends today."

"You have. They'll rejoice right along beside you when you regain your eyesight."

She rubbed away evidence of her tears. "I've always prided myself on not crying at the drop of a hat. But I seem to be making up for all those years I didn't."

"A lot has happened to you. Besides, there's nothing wrong with a good cry. Cleanses the soul."

"Well, mine must be sparklingly clean, then."

Colin chuckled. "Ready to go back out there?"

"Yes, Amber wanted me to meet one of her friends." She lowered her voice to a whisper. "I think it's a guy she's quite taken with. She mentioned him to me. Are you prepared for that?"

"I've taken a crash course in it with Tiffany's frequent boyfriends. I think she has a different one every month."

With Colin leading the way, Emma started for the door into the rec hall. "Not Amber?"

"No, this would be her first one. Who is it?"

"Neil Logan."

"Ah, the sheriff's son. He's a nice kid. I didn't know Amber was interested in him."

"She hasn't come right out and said that, but she mentions him a lot when we talk."

Just inside the rec hall, the noise level more sedate than before, Colin leaned close and said, "I've noticed Amber goes over to Grace's every afternoon to see you."

"Yeah, she's been helping me find my way around the house and honing my other senses. I think it began because she wanted to do something for me because of the computer. Now we end up talking more than anything."

"I'm glad. She's never done many activities after school like Tiffany."

"I think she's going to help Grace and me with baking cookies tomorrow. My first cooking lesson. That should be interesting. Even with my eyesight, I never was very good in the kitchen."

"Here comes Amber with Neil and J.T."

His whispered words tickled Emma's neck and she smiled. "How do they look together?"

"You're asking me, the father?" Colin said in mocked panic, pulling away a few inches.

"Emma, I want you to meet Neil Logan," Amber said.

She held out her hand and felt a large one close about hers. "It's nice to meet you, Neil."

"I'm so glad you're all right. I was in the car when the reverend hit—"

The teenager's voice came to an abrupt halt. Emma widened her smile, saying, "I appreciate your concern. I understand you're one of the leaders of the youth group."

"Yes, ma'am." Relief flowed through Neil's voice.

Amber and Neil stayed for a few minutes longer discussing some of the projects the youth group were going to do in the coming months.

When they left, Emma asked J.T., "Any news?"

"Nothing new. So far, no strangers have turned up in the area who are suspicious."

"So they might not be hanging around?"

"Yeah. But I'm still having a patrol car come by every hour. Doesn't hurt to be cautious."

She felt Colin's arm brush up against hers as though he had moved in closer. "Colin and I are going back to Derek's apartment this afternoon. I need to start thinking about closing the place up."

"That's never easy. I'll keep you two informed if I learn anything."

"Thanks, J.T.," Colin said, entwining his fingers through hers. After the sheriff walked away, he asked in a tough-sounding Humphrey Bogart voice, "Are you ready to blow this joint? The highway's calling."

Emma laughed. "Don't tell me you were a frustrated actor in high school."

"And you were probably the drama critic."

The light tone begun in the rec hall carried through the hour drive to Derek's apartment building. On the elevator ride to the top floor Emma remained surprisingly calm while Colin entertained her with a few impressions of his favorite actors.

"You are a multitalented man," Emma said as she left the elevator and turned right toward her brother's apartment. She passed the key to Colin.

"Why thank you, ma'am. I aim to please." He inserted the key into the lock and pushed the door open.

Emma started into the apartment. Colin grabbed her by the shoulders to halt her progress, tension conveyed in his grasp. "What's wrong?"

"The place has been searched—like the cabin."

She brought her hand up to her mouth, smothering her gasp. "They came here, too," she whispered, chilled to the bone at the invasion. She should have realized this would happen, even with the tight security in the building. It emphasized the lengths these people would go to for whatever they were looking for.

Colin pulled her back into the hallway. He placed his mouth next to her ear and murmured, "Let's go downstairs and call the police. For all we know, they may still be inside."

Tension mounted on the endless ride down to the lobby. Her thoughts swirled as though caught in the middle of a tornado. Every once in a while a fragment was tossed out, only to be snatched back into the whirling winds, nothing making any sense in the jumbled mess.

Dazed, she stood back and let Colin deal with the security guards, who made the call to the police. One of them went up to Derek's apartment while she and Colin waited for the police to arrive. She sat on the couch in the lobby while Colin paced in front of her, the rhythmic sound of his footsteps punishing the tile floor from one end of the lobby to the other.

Had they found what they were looking for? For a brief moment Emma hoped they had. Then, her life could get back to normal—whatever that was. But that feeling only lasted for a few heartbeats before her anger took over. She wouldn't let her brother die for nothing. Whoever did this would pay for the crime.

If only I could remember. If only I could see!

"Did you get much sleep last night?" Grace asked while walking from the sink in the kitchen to the stove.

Emma slouched over the table, propping herself up with her chin in her palm while taking a sip of coffee, strong but delicious. "No. Every time I closed my eyes I saw what Derek's apartment must have looked like. Colin said just about everything was destroyed and trashed." She shivered. "Such violence. I'm glad I didn't see it."

"Yeah, Colin called me this morning. He was pretty shaken up over the incident. Speaking of calls, you received several yesterday afternoon."

Emma straightened. "I did. From whom?"

"Your father called several times."

Emma's heart plummeted. She didn't want to deal with her father on top of everything else.

"Brandon McDonel and Marcus Peterson called, too. They all wanted to know how you were doing. They were concerned and hoped you would call them back."

"I probably should call Brandon and Marcus back. I have to work with Marcus concerning my brother's business and I need to find out about the irregularities J.T. suspects with the company. As my brother's heir, I think I should have my accountant examine the books."

"And Brandon?"

The curiosity in Grace's voice coaxed a smile out of Emma. "He's just an old friend."

"Old as in sixty years old?"

"No, as in a longtime friend. We dated for a while. He was my brother's roommate in college all four years. He works at a bank, just promoted to vice president. He's come a long way from the south side of Chicago. Very smart man, driven to be president of Premier Bank of New York by the age of forty."

"Will he make it?"

"Probably. He went to Harvard on a scholarship and graduated at the top of his class."

"Do you want me to dial their numbers for you?"

"No, I can do it. Amber has been helping me practice using the phone. I'm getting quite good at it. By the way, when will Amber be over to help us with the cookies?"

"Right after school. That's two hours from now."

"Then I'd better get these calls made so I can be ready for my cooking lesson. I know Brandon's number. What is Marcus's?"

After Grace recited it, Emma scooted back her chair and rose, using the table as her starting point for making her way to the den, counting off the steps as she went. If she remained blind for much longer, she would need to check into getting a cane. She hadn't wanted to think about it, but it might become necessary, as well as have some formal mobility training. She wanted to be as independent as possible, therefore she had to be realistic.

In the den, sitting on the couch, she found the phone and slowly punched in Marcus's number. His secretary put her right through to her brother's partner.

"It's so good to hear your voice, Emma. I've been worried about you."

"I'm doing as well as to be expected. I wanted to tell you that my accountant, Adam Moore, will be contacting you to look over the books for the company. Before I make any decisions concerning Derek's estate, I need to know where everything stands." She didn't want to tip Marcus off about her and J.T.'s suspicions.

There was a long pause before Marcus said, "Sure. Have him call me. Is there anything else I can do for you?"

"No, I haven't made many plans yet."

"Are you thinking of remaining involved with the business?"

"I can't make any decisions until after the audit and things are settled with Derek's murder."

"Sure. I understand. I'll be expecting your accountant's call."

She quickly placed a call to Adam, directing him to audit the books immediately and get back with her as soon as he found out anything. She stressed the urgency of the matter. Then she picked up the phone for the third time and punched in Brandon's private number at the bank. He answered it on the second ring.

"How are you, Emma? I wish you were back in New York."

Hearing the familiarity in his voice, Emma released a sigh slowly before answering. "I don't know when I'll be back. Things are up in the air right now." There had been a time when she would have welcomed his interest—not now.

"I want to help. What can I do?"

"Nothing right now."

"I'm going to be in Chicago on business in a few days. I'd like to see you. I've missed you. I can come to Crystal Springs."

The persuasive, husky tone in his voice reminded Emma of when they had dated. His charismatic charm, used so well in the past, left her cold. Her vague image of Colin popped into her thoughts as she listened to Brandon discuss when he could be in Crystal Springs.

"Call me when you're in Chicago. I don't know what I'll be doing. So much depends on when my memory comes back completely, and also my eyesight."

"That makes sense. How's it going? I can imagine how hard it would be to have witnessed Derek's murder and not remember a thing."

"I'm remembering bits and pieces every day. I'm optimistic." She had to be, because she was determined to remember who shot Derek.

"Good. I'll give you a call after my meeting in Chicago."

After she hung up with Brandon, Emma's hand lingered on the receiver. She needed to return her father's call, remembering Colin's sermon from Sunday and the words in the Gospel According to Matthew.

For if ye forgive men their trespasses, your heavenly Father will also forgive you.

Could she make peace with her father?

Her hands trembled as she made a call to her father. Her body stiffened in anticipation of hearing his deep, graveled voice.

"I didn't know if you would call me back, Emma."

The uncertainty that imbued her father's opening remark shook her. She'd never heard that from him. At a loss for words, she grappled with what to say.

"Emma, are you still there?"

"Yes, Dad." A sigh came from him and further surprised her. "Was there a reason you called me?"

"Do I have to have a reason?"

"You always have in the past."

"I just wanted to make sure you were all right and safe. The woman you're staying with told me you're doing okay, but I wanted to hear it from you."

She nearly dropped the receiver and had to grip it tighter. "Her name is Grace Fitzpatrick," was all she could think of to say.

"She informed me she'd been in the army and had taught self-defense. She assured me you were safe. I would still feel better if you were here in Chicago with me."

The tears that were always so close to the surface lately sprang into her eyes. "I'll be fine here. The sheriff has a patrol car coming by the house every hour, and when Colin isn't working, he's usually over at his aunt's. I'm never alone."

"Colin's the minister?"

"Yes."

"He's the one who hit you with his car."

"Dad, don't start. He saved my life. If he hadn't been there, they would have finished me off."

"Emma—I—" Her father cleared his throat. "I know how close I came to losing both my children. No parent should outlive his child. I'm sorry…" His voice faded into the silence.

For just a second it had sounded as though her father really loved her. "Dad?" Sadness and regret engulfed her. When he didn't say anything, she asked, "Are you still there?"

"Yes, Emma."

Those two words were heavy with an emotion she hadn't thought her father capable of—love. Was it just wishful thinking or a real feeling? she wondered, afraid to ask for fear of the answer.

A muffled cough filled the void, then her father said, "I have to go. I'm late for a meeting. Please call if there's anything I can do for you. You just tell me and I can have my security people down there in under thirty minutes."

Emma could imagine the S&J helicopter swooping down on Crystal Springs and landing in Grace's large front yard. "Thanks, Dad, for the offer, but I'm fine, really. I'll talk to you later."

After disconnecting, Emma sat on the couch with her shoulders slumped forward and her chin resting on her chest. She couldn't remember a time her father had used the word "please" with her.

Lord, I've never prayed before. I'm not even sure how, but is it possible that my father loves me? Help me to forgive him and mend our relationship. Seeing Colin with his family only makes me want one, too. It's always been just Der—Derek and me, with our parents on the fringes of our lives. Now with Derek gone, I don't have anyone.

Emma buried her face in her hands, her fingers still quivering from the last phone call. So much of her life was falling apart around her, but in the center there was a light that seemed to grow brighter each day she was in Crystal Springs. Hope dangled before her, just out of reach—much like her lost memories.

"The recipe calls for another cup of flour," Grace announced, thrusting a metal cup into Emma's hand. "Here, measure it while I set the oven to preheat."

"I don't know how." Even though she couldn't see, Emma stared at the object cradled in her palm as though it were an alien artifact.

"The flour canister is right in front of you. Dip it in and fill it all the way to the top, then I'll show you how to level the excess off."

Emma glanced over her shoulder in the direction of Amber. "Is she always this way?"

The teenager laughed. "Afraid so. You could be stuck chopping up the nuts."

"Hey, I'll change jobs."

"Girls, please. We have to bake three dozen in the next hour and a half. While I'm making the sugar cookie recipe, you can do the chocolate chip one. It's really very easy."

"Not if you can't cook," Emma shot back as she scooped the cup into the flour, patting the overflow until Grace touched her.

"You don't pack flour." She gave Emma a butter knife and helped her to level the ingredient to exactly one cup.

As Emma dumped it into the large bowl, the scent of flour teased her nostrils along with some of the other ingredients—vanilla and brown sugar. She'd never thought of the staples—sugar and flour—as having a smell, but then she had never used them to cook something.

"Now stir those dry ingredients together, then we'll add them to the wet ones."

"We...as in, you're gonna help me?"

"I'll add the dry while you use the mixer." Grace opened a drawer then slid it close.

From the sounds the older woman was making she must be setting up the mixer. A few seconds later Grace placed something into her hand.

"That's a rubber spatula. You'll use it to scrape the sides of the bowl while the mixer is doing its thing."

After positioning herself in front of the mixer, Emma stuck the spatula into the bowl and turned on the appliance. Grace began pouring the dry ingredients into the mixing bowl. The dough became harder and harder to combine.

"This isn't easy," she said, chuckling at the picture she must be projecting, especially with more ingredients on her and the counter than in the cookie dough.

"You still have to put the chocolate chips and the nuts in and mix them up." Grace switched off the mixer and set the bowl on the counter. "The chips are in a bag to your right. Amber, are you through with the pecans?"

"Yeah."

Emma sensed the teenager's approach from the left. She was getting good at feeling people's presence even when they didn't make a sound, as though she were attuned to a change in the air. She couldn't explain it but was glad she wasn't always getting surprised when someone came near her.

When the dough was finished, Emma and Amber both spooned it onto two cookie sheets. The teen opened the oven and a hot blast of air hit Emma in the face. She decided she had learned enough that day and gave the first baking sheet to Amber to put into the oven.

Emma dusted off her hands, positive that flour was flying everywhere. In fact, she was sure she had it all over her. But she felt good. Her mouth watered in anticipation of tasting the first dish she'd made. The scent of baking cookies added to all the other smells bombarding her.

"You did good, Emma," Grace said right before she turned on the mixer to prepare her dough. "Now all that's left is the cleanup."

"You mean little elves don't come in and do it for you?"

"Ha! I wish," Grace said, over the sound of the mixer.

"I'll wash. You can dry." Amber began stacking the dishes into the sink.

Emma listened to the activity around her and could tell what each one was doing by the sounds. She could even tell who was who by their scent. Amber liked to wear a light fragrance with a hint of lilac while Grace had on a perfume that smelled like a bouquet of roses.

Emma knew the second Colin came into the kitchen even though she hadn't heard the front door opening or closing. His distinctive scent was fresh like the woods she'd played in as a little girl.

"What brings you over here?" Drying a metal mixing bowl, Emma smiled toward Colin as he crossed the kitchen, the sound of his footfalls indicating he wore tennis shoes.

"Baking cookies. Someone needs to be the taster before you two take them to the ladies meeting tonight. I volunteer. It's a dirty job but someone's got to do it."

"Sorry, Dad. I've already got the job. Better luck next time."

"So that's why you hurried over here after school?"

The sound of a slap preceded Grace declaring, "Leave that cookie dough alone."

"But you know how much I like it."

Emma chuckled at the pout in Colin's voice. "I have to admit I like it better than the baked cookies, too."

"Here, Dad. You can lick this beater."

"At least, my daughter looks after me."

Listening to Colin's obvious delight at cleaning off the beater, Emma laughed even more. "You're definitely a loud eater."

"Aren't there two beaters?" he asked innocently.

"Sorry, Dad. I've already washed it."

Colin snapped his fingers. "If I hadn't answered the phone before leaving, I could have made it in time."

Emma felt Colin move into her personal space. Her heart reacted with a quickening beat.

"Which brings me to why I came over here. J.T. called about what the police in Central City discovered concerning the break-in at your brother's apartment."

Emma tensed, the past hour of fun suddenly coming to an end. Life intruded, and even though she wanted to find Derek's killers, for a brief moment she wanted the past hour back. She'd felt a part of a family and she liked that feeling.

"What did the police find?"

"Not much. They're thinking it's a professional job

since they had to get by the electronic security system, which we both know is a good one."

"Obviously not good enough," Grace said from the direction of the stove as she opened the oven door and the aroma of chocolate chip cookies intensified in the air.

"As you can imagine, the police aren't sure if anything is missing."

Emma leaned back against the counter, the day's activities catching up with her. "And I can't help them. I can't see a thing!"

The feel of Colin's hand on her arm conveyed his silent support as only he could. "Would you know what was missing even if you could see? You haven't been in his place in a year."

"Yes. Maybe." She sank more against the counter. "I don't know. But, at least, I could try."

His fingers weaved through hers. "It will happen."

"When? When the killers have escaped?"

"They may already be gone."

"Because they found what they're looking for?"

"It's a possibility we have to face."

She dropped her head, wishing she could see the tiles that Grace had told her were cream colored. "I'm not even sure we would know it if we saw it. What could be so important that my brother was killed for it?" She raised up her chin. "Don't answer that. I know there are many things that people value more than a human life."

"Sad, but true." Grace came toward Emma and put something down on the counter next to the sink.

"When are we going to the meeting?" Emma asked, groping for the next item to dry.

"In a couple of hours. Why don't you rest? I'll help Amber finish cleaning up in here." Grace took the towel from Emma and gently pushed her toward Colin. "See that she lies down."

"Hey, you two. I can take care of myself."

"I have no doubt about that," Grace said in a serious tone. "But you can't see yourself. I can, and you look tired."

"Are you telling me I don't look good?" Emma faced the older woman with her hands on her hips.

"Yup. That's what I'm saying. I always knew you were sharp, Emma St. James."

She chuckled. "You've only known me for a week."

"And in that time I've come to that conclusion."

Colin nudged Emma with his elbow. "Cut your losses. I've never been able to win with Grace."

Emma let out a long breath. "Okay. I *am* tired. I could use a nap. Will you set the alarm for me, Colin? I don't want to sleep more than an hour and a half." Not waiting for him, she started across the kitchen, keeping track of the steps she had taken.

He came up behind her. "You sure are getting independent."

She threw a smile over her shoulder. "Amber and Grace have been helping me. Every day I'm learning more and more about how to get around in here. I've mastered the downstairs. The past few days I've been working on the second floor and Amber even showed me the basement in case I decide to do any laundry."

"You want to do your own laundry?"

"I might. I want to help Grace as much as possible while I'm here."

"Yeah, well, don't do what I did once. I'm now the proud owner of several pink T-shirts and they aren't my daughters'."

Emma laughed, picturing Colin wearing one of his laundry mistakes.

"How did the cooking lesson go?"

She paused in the hallway outside her bedroom. "Not too bad. I suspect I still have some flour on me."

Colin stepped closer and brushed his fingers across her cheek. "Just a little."

She fought the urge to lean into his touch. So much was happening in her life, and she didn't know how to deal with these feelings he generated in her. She pulled back, grasping behind her for the door frame. "I appreciate you setting my alarm. I want to take extra care to look nice tonight. Some of the ladies have been so kind to me." She was still amazed that so many were praying for her.

Colin walked toward the nightstand. "Ninety minutes." Clicking sounds cut into the silence. "You're all set."

When he rejoined her at the doorway, Emma stood to the side to allow him by, not sure what to say to him. Finally she simply said, "Thank you."

"See you later."

His parting words left her happy and sad at the same time. What was going on with her? This wasn't the time or the place to lose her heart. It would never work. Her emotions lay bare and frightened her more than anything, more than facing blindness. How could anything be real when they came from all that was happening? His feelings came from guilt over hitting her. Did hers come from gratitude? She didn't know what was real.

* * *

The insistent beeping of her alarm jolted Emma awake. She fumbled for it, blissfully turning it off. She hated that sound and usually didn't set an alarm. "Why didn't I just ask Colin to call me?" she muttered, then instantly knew the answer. She didn't want to be any more of a burden to him than she already was.

Swinging her legs over the edge of the bed, she sat, searching with her feet for her shoes then sliding into them when she found them. She pushed her hair out of her face and hooked it behind her ears. What to wear to a meeting of the ladies at the church? Jeans? A dress?

Crash!

Emma jerked her head up, staring in the direction of the door. What was that? Was Grace all right?

Emma pushed off the bed and headed for the door. Opening it partway, she cocked her head and listened. The unnatural silence stilled her movements. Then she heard the sound of footsteps in the kitchen and low murmurs. Two people? She swung the door wider, leaning out into the hallway. Did Grace have a visitor? Was Colin still here?

She started for the kitchen.

A gruff masculine voice saying "Will you shut up" halted Emma's steps. She knew that voice. She'd heard those very words recently. Backing up, she groped for the entrance into her bedroom. Something was terribly wrong.

Chilled to the marrow of her bones, she swung around and raced across the room to the nightstand where the phone was. When she put the cold plastic against her ear, the quiet taunted her. No dial tone. Nothing! The receiver dropped from her numb fingers, landing on the bed. And her cell was in her purse in the kitchen, where she'd left it earlier.

She pivoted, facing the door. The feeling of being trapped quaked her to her core.

NINE

Emma's black world came crashing down on her. Panic and indecision held her immobile as she strained to listen for any sound of approaching footsteps.

Hide. Now!

Those two words propelled her into action. She raced for the door, her outstretched hands seeking any objects in her path. Maybe she could make it out the front before they saw her.

"What if she ain't here?" came a high-pitched male voice from the living room right off the foyer.

Emma froze. Trapped. She remembered that voice in the woods. Its cadence flashed a memory of hiding in the bushes, so terrified that she would be found.

"She's here. I've been watching."

The chilling words choked her with renewed terror. She turned her head from side to side as though scanning the hall for a hiding place when in reality all she could see was a black wall before her eyes.

Go back to my room? Hide under the bed? In the closet?

She shook those places from her thoughts. Too obvious. Then she remembered the door to the basement at the other end of the hallway. Without another second's hesitation she backtracked and went past her bedroom, trailing her hand along the wall until she encountered the doorjamb.

"Let's check downstairs first, then upstairs," the gruff voice said. "She's probably hiding since that lady knocked over the chair."

Grace! What have they done?

"Yeah, but she's blind. She's can't go too far. We'll get her."

The almost feminine sounding voice grated down Emma's spine as it had in the woods. Quietly she eased open the basement door and slipped inside, turning the lock. It wouldn't keep them out for long, but anything that slowed them down gave her hope someone would come.

Poised on the top stair, she tried to recall the day before when Amber had given her the tour. For a few seconds she couldn't think of a thing as fright erased her memories. All she could concentrate on was the heavy thud of footsteps advancing through the first floor, getting closer and closer to the basement door. Then the incessant ringing of Grace's cell in her purse by the front door vied for her attention. Muffled voices followed, then silence for a moment. Hope flared. Maybe they would leave. Footfalls started again, coming down the hall.

With her hands on the banister, she descended the steps into the musty-smelling room where the washer, dryer and furnace were located. Not a lot of places to hide. Four feet into the center Emma remembered the light that dangled from the ceiling. If she could unscrew the bulb, then if they came down here, at least they would be in the dark like her. Where had Amber said it was? Closer to the washer and dryer?

Flinging her arms in the air, she moved toward the far wall and discovered the single light. With trembling hands, she took it out of the socket, the bulb slipping from her fingers and crashing to the cement floor. The sound echoed in the dank, small basement, shooting a fresh wave of fear through her.

Hide!

She groped for the washer, hearing the crunch of glass beneath her shoes. She touched the appliance's smooth surface, then slid her hand along the edge until she came to the metal shelves. On the other side a space big enough to fit her body into beckoned. She squeezed into it and waited, her labored breathing reverberating through her mind.

Colin hunkered over his desk in his study, scribbling some ideas for a sermon on a pad. His mind kept wandering to Emma and the past week. Finally in frustration he gave up and dropped his pencil on the nearly blank piece of paper.

Leaning back in his chair, he combed his hands through his hair and stared up at the ceiling, trying to bring order to his chaotic thoughts concerning Emma.

He'd been happily married once and knew what a good marriage was like. He'd never really envisioned falling in love again, and yet the feelings forming for Emma reminded him suspiciously of love. How could that be possible in such a short time? He and his wife had been high school sweethearts and had known each other for years before marrying. They'd had the same deep faith in the Lord. Neither was true with Emma and him. But every time he was around her, all he could think of was having a future with her.

Lord, I don't know what to do. I can't seem to stop these feelings from developing. But I don't see it working. What do You want me to do?

Resting his elbows on his desk, he scrubbed his hands down his face, weary. The mad pace of the past week hunched his shoulders and sagged his head.

The blare of the phone next to him jerked him upright. He snatched it up. "Hello."

"Colin, this is Linda. I've been trying to get hold of Grace, but her line is busy, has been for the past fifteen minutes. I even tried her cell phone. No one answered. Our meeting has started. With all that's been going on I was kind of worried. She's always on time."

Colin's grip strengthened about the plastic receiver. "I'll go over and see what's going on."

After hanging up, he bolted to his feet and strode to the window that faced Grace's house. Lights blazed from almost every room on the first floor and his aunt's car was still in the driveway. Something wasn't right. He felt it in his gut. Quickly he picked up the phone and punched in the number of the sheriff's office.

When J.T. came on the line, Colin said, "Grace and Emma didn't show up at the ladies meeting. Something's going on at the house. I'm going in."

He dropped the receiver into its cradle while J.T. was shouting for him to stay put. That wasn't going to happen. He knew firsthand how important every minute—every second—could be in a situation like this.

Colin raced out the back door and across his yard, his

heartbeat thumping against his chest at a mad pace. Using his key, he let himself into Grace's kitchen. The sight of his aunt stretched out on the tile floor seized his breath. Kneeling next to Grace, he felt for a pulse at her neck and released the trapped air in his lungs with a sigh. She was alive.

But is Emma?

That question drove him to his feet. He heard movement above him in two different rooms. Good, that meant they hadn't found her yet or they wouldn't still be searching.

All his earlier training came rushing back to him. First, he needed to check Emma's bedroom. If she wasn't there, he would take care of the two upstairs then find her—he hoped—before the intruders did.

He slipped off his shoes so his footsteps would be silent. Making his way to Emma's room on the first floor, he searched every place she could have hidden, seeing evidence—closet in disarray, the bedspread lifted—that the men in the house had been there before him.

The slamming of a door above him drew him back into the hallway. Something heavy crashed to the floor. They were getting angry. Good. That could work in his favor.

"She ain't here," a high-pitched male voice said at the top of the landing.

"She is, Manny. I'll recheck up here. You go downstairs. Get that door open if you have to bust it down, then search whatever is behind it. And make sure that lady is still out cold."

Prodding steps resonated through the house as Colin glimpsed a short, stocky man coming down the stairs. In Manny's hand a semiautomatic gleamed, riveting Colin's full attention. He pressed back against the wall next to the entrance into the living room and waited for the man to enter on his way to the kitchen to check on Grace.

Noises from above bombarded Emma. She crouched lower, curling herself into a ball while her pulse beat so rapidly she felt faint. Although she had locked the basement door, she knew that wouldn't keep them out for long. They had tried it once and moved on for the time being. They would be back when she wasn't discovered anywhere else.

Lord, help me. Please. I'm so worried about Grace. Is she alive? I might not be worthy but she is. Please help her, at least.

Colin inched closer as the sound of the man grew nearer. He'd only have one chance. Emma and Grace's lives depended on him succeeding. A foot inside the living room, Manny halted and began to twist toward Colin, raising his gun.

With lightning speed, Colin leaped forward, bringing his hand down on Manny's arm. The semiautomatic clanked to the area rug a few feet beyond the entrance, masking its sound somewhat. The short, stocky man fell to the right, going after the weapon. Colin followed, throwing his full weight on top of Manny.

Their rolling bodies knocked into an end table, the lamp smashing to the hardwood floor. In the distance Colin heard running footsteps coming down the upstairs hall. He only had seconds before the other intruder would be on top of him.

With a strength born out of desperation, Colin broke

free of the bear hug Manny had him in and pushed back, lifting his fist and slugging the man. He hammered his balled hand into Manny's face until he went limp.

The man above came crashing down the stairs, yelling, "Manny, where are you? Did you find her?"

Snatching up the gun, Colin jumped to his feet, rotating as a tall, thin man charged into the living room, his weapon poised in front of him.

Lord, forgive me. Colin aimed and fired at the same time the second intruder got off a shot.

Two shots thundered through the terrorizing silence. Emma trapped the scream inside her. Every inch of her shook. She clasped her hands together and bowed her head. *Please, Lord, protect Grace.* Then an even scarier thought invaded her mind. What if Colin was upstairs? What if—

She heard some noise as though people moved around on the first floor. She curled herself into the smallest ball possible as far back into the corner as she could go and waited.

Five minutes.

Ten minutes.

Someone tried the handle to the basement door. Muted voices drifted to her, then the sound of a key being inserted into the lock. The door swung open and light flooded down the stairs.

Emma blinked. Light? She saw it! Elation at regaining her sight pushed her fear to the side for a few seconds until footfalls pounded down the wooden steps, drawing her full attention to the stairs.

"Emma? Are you down here?"

The sweetest voice in the whole world pierced through the thudding of her heartbeat in her ears. She sprang up and rushed toward Colin, launching herself into his arms at the bottom of the stairs.

A fleeting image of the man burned itself into her mind as she buried herself in his embrace, sobs shaking her. "I—I—thought you—were them."

"J.T. has them in handcuffs upstairs. You're safe now."

Emma drew back, Colin's face in the shadows thrown by the light coming from the first floor. "Grace? Is she all right?"

"Other than being furious and having one terrific headache, yes. What about you?"

"I can see you!"

He stepped back into the light flowing from above, and for the first time, she saw Colin. Her breath caught at the handsomeness of his dark features. It shouldn't have surprised her, because of his gentle, caring nature, but his perfection did shock her. He'd played down his appearance so she had concluded he had been plain looking. He was anything but plain, which endeared him to her even more. Not because of his attractive features but because it hadn't mattered to him. In her life and profession a person's looks had been everything. She'd often been surrounded by people who obsessed about their appearance. With Colin, she had been forced to explore beyond that.

He arched a black brow. "You aren't normally speechless."

Tears glistened in her eyes, making his image blurry. "You are so beautiful."

"*I* am?" he exclaimed, dismay descending over his features.

She chuckled, took a step closer to him and laid her hand along his strong jaw, stroking its length. "No, I don't mean your looks, but your soul. You don't need me to tell you that you're handsome, but you should hear from me how good you are. You saved my life a second time."

He flushed beneath her fingertips. "I—I—" He snapped his mouth closed.

She caressed his full lips, staring at them as they curved slowly into a mischievous grin.

"You'd better stop that. We have probably the whole sheriff's department upstairs. I wouldn't want to shock anyone in my congregation."

"Why, Reverend Fitzpatrick, whatever do you have in mind?"

"This."

He dragged her to him, flattening her up against him while he kissed her. She raised up on tiptoes and wound her arms around him, wanting to get as close as possible. His warmth chased away the chill that had been embedded in her bones when the intruders broke in.

When he drew back, his forehead touched hers and his hands cradled her face. "I want you to look at the two men before the sheriff takes them away. One has been shot and will go to the emergency room. The other has a few cuts and bruises on his face." One corner of his mouth quirked up. "I'm afraid I got a little overzealous in subduing him. Maybe one of them will trigger a memory."

"I remember both their voices. They were the same ones I heard in the woods."

"Then maybe you can identify them as your brother's killers." He took her hand out of habit and led the way up the stairs to the first floor.

Emma blinked at the brightness of the light the closer she came to the entrance into the basement. Voices coming from the living room penetrated her world. She had been in the dark for so long both figuratively and literally, that it took her a moment to get her bearings.

Colin started for the front. She hung back, suddenly apprehensive about seeing Derek's murderers. What if she couldn't positively identify them? What if she didn't remember them as the ones in the cabin? She recalled her flight through the woods, the voices, even running out onto the highway and Colin's SUV coming toward her. But before that was still a blank.

The warmth of Colin's grasp and his comforting expression anchored her and gave her the strength she needed to confront the two men who most likely murdered her brother.

God will be with you. Those words materialized in her mind and grew with each step she took toward the living room. Serenity calmed the rapid beat of her heart and she knew everything would be all right, even if she didn't remember at this time. She wasn't alone.

A few feet inside the room, Emma saw a tall, thin man holding a bloody towel to his forearm. His dark gaze lifted to hers and she was whisked back to the cabin. She stood outside looking into the window near the door. Her brother sat in a chair with his hands tied behind his back. The tall, thin man hovered over him. He struck Derek over and over, demanding something from her brother. Then she glimpsed the gun in the hand of the other intruder, a short, bulky man who appeared to work out a lot. The weapon's report staggered her as though she had been shot. The tall man's gaze was riveted to hers with such coldness in his eyes she couldn't understand how she could have forgotten him.

Emma shook the memory from her thoughts, focusing on the present, on the tall man still staring at her. There was something she was forgetting. But what? Nothing came to mind.

While Colin explained to J.T. that she had regained her eyesight, she swung her attention to the other intruder, handcuffed, with a deputy next to him. The short man didn't look her way. He kept his face averted.

Turning toward J.T., she said through clenched teeth, "They're the ones." She pointed to the shorter one. "He's the one who pulled the trigger."

"That's all we need right now. Colin can bring you down to the station and you can give your statement tomorrow." J.T. nodded to his deputies to take the two outside.

"Where's Grace?" Emma asked, searching the couple of people left in the living room.

"One of my men took her to the hospital to be checked out. She didn't want to go, but I insisted."

Colin chuckled. "That was quite an accomplishment. Grace rarely does what she doesn't want to do. Very stubborn."

"Some say I can have quite a stubborn streak, too. I guess she met her match." J.T. closed his pad and slid it into his shirt pocket.

"Or Grace is more hurt than you think," Emma said, and edged toward the front door, her worry making her anxious. "Colin, let's go to the hospital."

"You two go on. We have some more work to do

here." J.T. waved them away. "But I'll see both of you first thing tomorrow morning."

Five minutes later Colin headed the short distance to the regional hospital. At a four-way stop sign he slanted a look toward Emma. She rested her head back against the seat, staring out the side window.

"Okay?" he asked, concerned with all that she had been through in the past week and a half.

She swiveled her head toward him and smiled, the illumination from a streetlight casting a golden glow on her features. "I will be once I know Grace is all right."

"Her head's too hard to have any lasting effects," Colin said as much to reassure himself as Emma.

"I hope you're right. If anything happened to Grace because of me, I don't know if I could—" Emma didn't finish her sentence.

Instead she peered out the window again, letting the silence expand between them. Colin couldn't blame her. He'd once been trained in combat, and he felt overwhelmed with all that had transpired since her brother's death. It was a lot to assimilate for anyone. His admiration for Emma grew each day.

Thinking back to that split second when he had to decide whether to shoot the tall, thin man, he was thankful his accuracy hadn't faltered over the years, because he had taken a risk and aimed not for the chest but the smaller target of his lower arm, which held his gun. Even doing that had left Colin shaken, producing flashes of memory of the Gulf War and a time when he had killed.

Thank You, Lord, for sparing me reliving taking a man's life, no matter how much he may have deserved it. I would have, if need be, to protect Emma and Grace, but I'm glad I didn't have to. He knew he would have to live with the realization he would have killed again, but he wouldn't allow the guilt to take hold as it had years before during the Gulf War. Now he knew the power of the Lord's forgiveness.

As Colin pulled into the hospital lot, Emma said, "There's something about that tall man that bothers me."

"He killed your brother."

"No, it's more than that." Her gaze met his. "I can't put my finger on it. I should be remembering something important."

"Something that happened at the cabin?"

"Maybe." She clasped her head. "I hate this not remembering. When will my life return to normal?"

"Honestly?" Colin parked his SUV near the emergency entrance. "I don't know that it ever will. You've gone through a lot. You've lost someone very important to you. That changes you."

"Because you know firsthand with the death of your wife?"

"Yes. Mary Ann died four years ago, and I thought my life had come to an end. We had been high school sweethearts, and when I married her, I thought we would grow old together. Thankfully I had Amber and Tiffany. They needed me so I couldn't dwell too long in self-pity. I turned to the Lord and asked for His help. Two days later Grace showed up in Crystal Springs for a two-week vacation. Not six months after that, she retired and moved in next door."

"She's quite a lady."

"Yup. She took us under her wing and has become

like a second mother to the girls. There are times I have no idea what to say to my two daughters, but Grace does. It's nice having a woman's perspective for Amber and Tiffany."

Colin exited his car and came around to open Emma's door. She'd already climbed from the front seat.

"I keep forgetting you have your eyesight back," he said with a grin, falling into step beside her.

"When the doctor first told me it was all in my mind, I didn't believe him. I wanted to see. But not until I was down in that basement, listening to everything going on upstairs and not knowing what was happening, did I *really* want to see. I just didn't know I could, since it was so dark, until you opened the door."

"I'm glad you didn't know. I wouldn't have wanted you to try something because you could see."

"Like one of those moves Grace showed me?"

"Yeah. I wonder how they got the drop on her."

"Maybe we shouldn't say anything. I figure she'll be pretty upset about that."

Colin opened the door into the hospital and let Emma go first. "Knowing Grace, she'll bring it up."

The nurse at the counter directed Colin to a room on the first floor of the two-story hospital. He and Emma waited until the doctor finished with Grace before entering.

She swung her legs over the edge. "It's about time y'all got here. Let's go home."

Colin held up his hands. "Hold it. Didn't I hear the doctor tell you he wanted to keep you overnight for observation?"

"If he wants to observe me, he'll have to come to my

house. I'm not staying here." She stood and immediately grasped the edge of the bed.

"See, you aren't ready to leave," Emma said, reaching out to help Grace.

His aunt's eyes widened. "You got your sight back?"

Emma nodded.

"Why didn't anyone tell me?"

"You were already on your way here when we came up from the basement. That's where Emma was hiding." Colin assisted Grace in sitting down again on the bed.

"Smart move." Grace beamed, turning her full smile on Emma. "Sugar, this is wonderful news!"

"Yeah, it's about time."

Colin heard Emma's vulnerability behind her retort. Even though she grinned, he saw the flat dullness in her eyes and the tired set of her shoulders.

"Well, as soon as we reach home, we need to celebrate." Grace slowly rose again, wincing halfway up. Wobbling, she stopped.

"Grace," Colin said, putting his arm around her to steady her. "You *are* staying here tonight and I don't want an argument."

"But who'll stay with Emma?"

Emma thought of what had happened in Grace's house not an hour before, and she wasn't sure if she would sleep a wink, but there was no way she would let Grace come home in the condition she was in. "I can stay by myself."

Both Grace and Colin said, "No."

"What do you mean no? I'm not blind and I'll have you two know that I've been living by myself for years." With her hands on her waist, Emma forced a stern tone into her voice, glancing from aunt to nephew.

"Have you forgotten already what almost happened tonight?" For the second time Colin assisted Grace onto the bed, then faced Emma.

"Believe me, I remember every second, but those two are in jail so they can't hurt me anymore."

"What about the person who hired them?" Grace eased back against the pillow, closing her eyes for a few seconds.

"I don't think—I mean—I—" Emma sighed. "I should be fine for the night. I doubt he would do anything so quickly after what went on at your house."

"He?" Colin's brows rose.

"Okay, she, he, it. Whoever was behind everything." Frustration, ever present, flooded Emma, and she wanted to do something irrational like scream.

"Why don't you stay at my house for the night? Amber has been dying to show you her room. She has twin beds. You can use one of them. In fact, my two girls will probably fight over whose room you'll share."

"Then tomorrow, first thing, y'all can come pick me up." Grace's forehead crunched up as though she was in pain.

"Do you need anything?" Emma came closer, worried about the woman who had taken her in and become a friend.

Grace waved her hand. "No, I'll be fine. The doctor gave me some pain medication, which should be kicking in at any moment."

The mention of pain medication doubled Emma's heartbeat. She remembered her fight to shake the habit and never wanted anyone to go through what she had. "Be careful, Grace."

The older woman laughed shakily. "It takes more than a bump on the head to get me down for long. I still can't believe they took me by surprise when I carried the cookies out to the car. When they forced me into the house because they wanted me to show them where you were, I saw my opportunity. I had the short guy on the floor, but the other one hit me with his gun. As I passed out, I took the chair with me, hoping you heard the noise."

"I did! That saved my life."

Grace's intense gaze caught hers. "No, your quick thinking saved your life. You'll be teaching a class on self-defense before too long."

"I think I'll leave that to you."

"It didn't do me much good tonight."

"Kinda hard to defend yourself against a gun," Colin said with a twinkle in his eyes. "We'd better leave you to get some rest. We'll be back first thing tomorrow."

Grace shifted on the bed. "What I mean by first thing is six in the morning," she called out as they left.

Out in the hall Colin chuckled. "But that's not what I mean. I'll give her until nine."

"You don't think she'll call you before that."

"Probably. Maybe I won't answer."

"Oh, you're a tricky one."

"We'll need to go by the police station first, anyway. I want to make our statements before picking up Grace. I don't want to see those two out on the street."

Emma shivered, hugging her arms to her, remembering the cold look in the tall one's eyes, as though human life meant nothing to him. But tomorrow she would ask J.T. if she could see the man again. She had to remember what was nagging her.

* * *

The dark shadows of night gave way to the gray of dawn. Emma stood at the window in the kitchen, staring at Grace's house, a short distance from Colin's. She cradled a mug of awful-tasting coffee and took several sips of the hot brew, wrinkling her nose as she drank it. Nothing seemed to warm her insides, not even this foul blackened water. She really needed to learn to cook.

A sound above her told her someone was up and moving around. The day was beginning and soon she would have to face her brother's murderers.

Last night she hadn't slept at all. After talking to Tiffany and Amber for an hour, she had tried to lie down, but every time she'd closed her eyes she'd seen her brother being murdered again. Finally, around four in the morning, she'd crept from Amber's bedroom and down the stairs, careful not to wake anyone. She was exhausted, but she couldn't stop from thinking and replaying all that had happened.

Grace's car stood sentinel next to the house. That was where everything had started last night. When Emma thought about the terror that had gripped her, she also remembered the prayers she'd offered to God. She recalled the peace she had experienced when she had walked toward the living room and Derek's killers. It had felt as if the Lord had walked with her. Is that what Colin meant? With God, you weren't ever alone?

"Did you get any sleep last night?" Colin's deep voice penetrated her musing.

She twisted around, her hands still cupping her mug, trying to draw some warmth into her. "No."

"I'm so sorry, Emma. I know none of this is easy."

"I have remembered something." She came toward him. "I know that tall man."

TEN

"Who is he?" Colin headed for the coffeepot, sitting on his kitchen counter.

"Don't. It tastes bad. You probably should make some more."

Emma offered him a small smile, still not used to *seeing* him. His dark hair lay at odd angles, as though he had run his fingers through it instead of combing it. She fought the urge to straighten it, curling her hands tighter around the mug.

"Emma!"

She blinked and realized she had been caught staring at him instead of answering.

"Who is he?"

"That I don't know. I just know I've seen him before my brother was murdered. I'm still trying to figure out where and when. I hope seeing him today will spark a memory."

"It'll come to you." Colin emptied the pot and then began preparing more coffee.

Emma watched him, his movements economical, nothing wasted. His hands were large with long, slender fingers. They were capable of beating up an intruder but also being so gentle and comforting to a lost soul.

She walked to the sink and poured the half-drunk coffee down the drain, relishing the scent of the new brew as it saturated the kitchen. "I hope you're right." She placed her mug next to the pot.

Colin relaxed back against the counter, his gaze sweeping down her length. "Do you want to get a change of clothes from Grace's?"

Emma chuckled. "Are you telling me I don't look good?"

His grin lit his whole face. "On the contrary. You look very good." A smoldering regard traveled down her. "I just figured you were tired of wearing the same clothes as yesterday. My daughters, especially Tiffany, manage to change several times a day."

Emma took in her attire of black slacks and animal-print blouse. "They have been through a lot." She gestured down her length. "Thankfully, they don't wrinkle easily—especially since I've slept in them—but I should probably change. I also want to make sure Grace's house is cleaned up before she comes home. Can we go over there before we go to the sheriff's office?"

"Yeah, since it's the crack of dawn, we should have plenty of time. I'll call J.T. to make sure he's through with the house and we can go in. But first I need some coffee." He shifted around and took a mug from the cabinet. After pouring Emma hers, he filled his. "I heard you and the girls talking."

"We didn't keep you up, did we?"

He shook his head. "I didn't go to sleep for quite a

while and then I don't think I slept more than an hour or so. It was good to hear you all laughing."

"You have great daughters. Tiffany had me in tears telling me about a chocolate-milk bomber. Some student at school has been tossing a carton of chocolate milk over the balcony every day after lunch and it busted all over the floor down below, making a mess. The principal laid a trap for the bomber, as the kids call the student, but he eluded it. No one knows who the student is, but every day a chocolate-milk carton is busted somewhere in the school."

"The pranks kids play." Colin sipped his coffee.

"I bet you did a few in your day."

"Who? Me? I was a perfect child."

His mischievous gleam told her otherwise. "Yeah, I bet. I'm going to have to talk to Grace and get the scoop on you."

The mischief curled his lips. "She doesn't know a thing."

"Have I ever told you that when my curiosity is aroused I don't let go until I find out what I want to know?"

"Nope. That's nice to know. Have I ever told you I was trained never to divulge national secrets?"

"Oh, I think you have challenged me."

"Yes, ma'am, I have." His smirk flashed over the rim of his mug as he took another drink.

She playfully punched him in the arm. "I didn't know you were such a rogue."

"There are many sides to me, Emma." His intense gaze snared hers.

The coldness inside her melted at the look he gave her. Each day she was with him she was discovering the truth in that statement. A man comfortable in many different situations. A man capable of such tenderness but also such fierceness, too. A man she could fall in love with.

A man who could break her heart.

Colin thrust open the back door to Grace's house and allowed Emma to enter first. She hesitated, then stepped through the threshold into the kitchen, her attention on the overturned chair next to the table in the middle of the room. Seeing the trembling in her hands, he took hold of them and halted her progress.

"We don't have to do this. You look fine the way you are."

She attempted a smile that faded instantly. "No, I won't let fear rule my life. And I won't let Grace come home to a messy house." Emma pulled her hands from his and bent over to right the chair, scooting it in flush with the table's edge as Grace had it every morning. "One room down and quite a few left." She glanced at him over her shoulder and this time her smile stayed.

Following Emma through the dining room into the living room, Colin came to a stop inside the doorway, looking for the bloodstain on the area rug near the foyer. *Lord, please forgive me for what I had to do to protect the ones I love. But I will not let anyone harm Emma or Grace.* Although he had told himself last night he wouldn't feel guilty for shooting Roy, he hadn't slept well, visions of the fight streaming across his consciousness and keeping him awake for hours. It would take some time, but he would deal with those feelings, with God's help.

"I'm not sure if that will come out." Emma pointed to the red on the navy-and-tan area rug.

"I doubt it, too. Let's take it up. I'll get Grace a new one."

"Good idea." Emma picked up one end of the coffee table while Colin took the other.

After setting it down out of the way, Colin rolled up the carpet and took it to the back porch. When he reentered the living room a few minutes later, he found Emma gone. Panic pounded his heart against his rib cage, and he started down the hall, searching for her.

"Emma! Where are you?"

"I'm changing. Be out in a sec," she called from her bedroom.

Relieved, he propped himself against the wall in the hall and waited for her to emerge. Crossing his arms over his chest, he tried to ignore the fear that gripped him from being back in this house after what had happened the night before. What if Linda hadn't called him about Grace and Emma not showing up for the meeting? What if he hadn't been successful in stopping those two men? What if Grace hadn't knocked over the chair and alerted Emma? As the "what ifs" trailed across his mind like a flashing banner on a Web site, his breathing grew shallow and his pulse thundered in his ears. He had come so close to losing two people who were very important to him.

When had his heart become so involved with Emma? Never before had he done anything without careful consideration. He didn't have an impulsive bone in his body, and yet with Emma, he couldn't seem to stop himself from falling in love with her—kind of like skydiving without a parachute. This wasn't going to end well, he thought as her door opened and he pushed himself away from the wall, mentally trying to prepare himself for the crash landing.

"A washed face and a change of clothes can do wonders. I almost feel human again."

He took in her blue jeans and hot-pink shirt, then rested on her freshly scrubbed face, one that had haunted his dreams every night since he had met her. "Let's finish straightening up, then get to the station. I bet Grace has called the house at least twice since we've been over here. I purposefully left my cell phone at home."

"Oh, you're so devious. Probably comes from those years spent playing pranks on others."

Winking at her, he walked toward the stairs. "Probably."

Ten minutes later Emma finished closing the last closet door, completing the cleanup job. Thankfully, there hadn't been too much of a mess. Grace could now come home, and except for the missing area rug, nothing seemed out of place.

As they left Grace's house, Emma said, "I need to return to New York. I can't keep sponging off your aunt. There's no reason for me to stay now that my vision's back."

Colin halted. "No reason! How about there's someone who hired those two thugs to kill your brother and you, too. Do you really think you're safe now? I'd call that a good reason not to go to New York and stay in your apartment alone."

"I can't put you and your family in any more danger. Look at what happened to Grace because of me. I need to leave just as soon as I know Grace is all right."

Colin's eyes grew round, then narrowed, the intensity in them unnerving. "Then take your father up on his offer of a bodyguard. I don't want you left unprotected. I—" He clamped his mouth shut and pivoted away, glaring off into space.

Tension vibrated off Colin, hitting her in waves. "I can't, Colin. I haven't taken anything from my father in years. If I have to I can hire someone, but—"

He spun around, gripped her arms and hauled her to him. "I will protect you. I started the job and I will finish it. The minute we find out who's behind this, you can hightail it to New York as fast as you can."

"But—"

He pressed his fingers across her mouth, stilling her flow of words. "Please, for me. If you left and something happened to you, I could never forgive myself for letting you walk away. For that matter, I know my aunt. She wouldn't be able to, either. Do you really want to do that to us after all we've done for you?"

"You're playing dirty. That's not fair. What about Amber and Tiffany? They could get caught up in all of this. I couldn't forgive myself if something happened to either one of them."

His chest expanded in a deep breath. "Okay, I can have them go stay with friends."

"You can't do that indefinitely."

He stepped back, plunging his hand through his hair. "I know, but something tells me this will be over soon. In less than two weeks you've regained your eyesight and remembered what happened at the cabin. We've got some solid leads and J.T. is a good investigator. He worked in homicide in Chicago before coming back home to Crystal Springs. Give it another week, then we'll talk about you leaving."

His tension infused itself in her, winding around her own nerves and making her rigid. She thought of returning to New York and her large apartment off Fifth Avenue. The lonely emptiness of her existence stretched out before her in a bleakness that left her numb.

"Please, Emma. We can renew our efforts to find out who is behind your brother's murder. There's always a chance one of those men will talk, cut a deal with J.T."

A tremor snaked down her spine when she thought of the tall man's cold, cold eyes. "No, somehow I don't think so."

Colin held out his hand. "Let's go to the station and find out."

She stared at him for a long moment then fit her hand in his. "We can always pray one of them did."

Colin paused, looked at her and said, "What a marvelous idea." He bowed his head and closed his eyes. "Dear Heavenly Father, please guide us to the one who had Derek murdered. Show us the way so justice can be done and our lives can return to normal. Amen."

"Amen," Emma murmured, suddenly wondering what in the world was normal anymore. She had the funny feeling her life had changed forever.

On the short drive to the sheriff's office, Emma remained quiet, trying to imagine her life in New York after all this was over. How was she going to manage to go on without Derek—without Colin? And where did God fit into her life? Was she worthy of His love as Colin said? She hadn't lived an exemplary life. She came to the Lord deeply flawed. Was it possible He could forgive her past sins?

An hour later Emma finished giving her statement to J.T., relieved that everything she had remembered the night before was even clearer this morning. She wanted there to be no doubt that those two thugs were the ones who had killed her brother.

"Are you ready, Emma?" J.T. asked, scraping his chair back and standing. "Roy Barnes is in the second interview room. You can observe from the other side of the two-way mirror. I doubt he'll say much, but if you can remember anything, let me know."

She nodded, her throat swelling with the thought of seeing the man again. But she had to do it. She had to try to remember what had been nagging her for the past twelve hours.

She waited on the other side of the mirror while J.T. and Madison went into the interview room. Colin came up beside her and faced forward as she did, watching. His hand fumbled for hers, and he held it tight between them.

Roy Barnes—the name didn't ring a bell with her—sat slouched over, studying his fingernails as if he was determining whether he needed a manicure. When J.T. switched on the tape recorder, Roy glanced toward the mirror, his eyes icy pinpoints. Emma sucked in a shallow breath. Suddenly she felt as though there was no glass between them and she and Roy were standing toe-to-toe.

"Okay?"

Colin's calm voice reassured her, easing some of the constriction about her chest. "Yes."

"Anything?"

"No."

After J.T. said the necessary information for the tape recording, he continued, "We have you cold on the attempted murder of Grace Fitzpatrick and Emma St. James, as well as the murder of Derek St. James. Who hired you?"

Roy laughed, a menacing sound that rocked Emma to her core. "I'm not saying a word until I've spoken to my lawyer. I know my rights."

"He's on his way." J.T. clicked off the tape recorder and rose. "We're gonna make a deal with the first one of you that talks. The other will be prosecuted to the full extent of the law. So think about that while you wait for your lawyer."

As the sheriff turned to leave, Emma caught his look of disappointment. "I didn't think it would be easy. Maybe the other guy will say something."

"While you were talking with J.T. earlier, Madison told me that Manny Stanovich lawyered up, too. You'd think they would want to make a deal."

Emma faced Colin. "Maybe they don't know who hired them."

"Or maybe they're too afraid to talk. Do you remember anything about him?" Colin nodded his head toward the mirror.

Emma stared at Roy, now picking at his fingernails, his expression calm and in control, as if he was waiting for a table at a restaurant. She closed her eyes and replayed her brother's murder, cringing when the gun went off in her mind. Tears crowded behind her eyelids.

She swallowed hard. "Nothing. Just this vague feel-

ing I've seen him before. That it's important somehow."
She heard J.T. and Madison behind her and spun around.
"You heard?"

"Yes." J.T. looked at the state investigator and added,
"Madison is going to dig into both Roy and Manny's
past. If anything turns up, we'll let you know."

Colin placed his hand on Emma's shoulder as he had
so often done when she couldn't see. His touch soothed
the knot of tension in her stomach. "We'd better go pick
up Grace before she decides to walk home."

"Knowing your aunt, that's a definite possibility,"
J.T. said with a chuckle.

Emma's head throbbed from trying to remember all
day long. But all that presented itself was a blank slate
when it came to Roy Barnes. She curled her legs under
her on the couch in Grace's den and rolled her shoulders to ease the tense set of her muscles. Leaning against
the cushioned arm, she cradled her chin in her palm and
watched Colin pace in front of the coffee table.

"Colin, stop. You're making me crazy." Grace set her
mug on the coaster on the end table next to her leather
lounge chair.

He paused, looked sheepishly at them then resumed
his pacing. "Sorry. Too much nervous energy." Rubbing
his hands together, he peered at the floor as he walked.
"We're missing something."

"It's probably staring us in the face, but for the life
of me I don't know what it is. Amber will call if she
comes up with anything on the Internet concerning
Manny and Roy, right?" Emma couldn't take her eyes
off Colin. He was wonderful to look at.

"Yes, but there are a lot of people with the name Roy Barnes. For all we know, that may not be his real name. Maybe J.T. or Madison will discover something." Colin loomed on the other side of the coffee table, curling and uncurling his hands, his arms hanging stiffly at his sides.

"Amber told me she was going to do some cross-referencing with Manny Stanovich. His name isn't as common." Wincing, Grace kneaded her right temple.

"Do you want something for that headache?" Emma asked for the third time that day since Grace had come home from the hospital.

"No, I try to avoid medication unless it's absolutely necessary. This—" Colin's aunt waved toward her head "—is a minor inconvenience."

Wishing she had been that wise after her car accident, Emma turned her gaze toward Colin, whose attention was fixed on her but without any recognition, as if he was deep in thought. "It certainly didn't sound like this was their first time working together, so cross-referencing might bring up something." When he didn't respond, she said, "Colin?"

He shook his head as though ridding his mind of cobwebs. "When do you think you'll hear back from your accountant?"

"I imagine in the next day or two. I told him it was a high priority. If he doesn't call soon, I'll call him."

"I think we should pay a visit to your brother's company."

"Why?"

"I don't know." He massaged the back of his neck. "Call it a gut feeling."

"Derek usually worked out of his apartment in Central City, but the main offices are in Chicago."

"Fine, we should go—"

The phone ringing interrupted Colin. He moved quickly and picked it up. "Hello?" There was a pause while the other person said something, then he stiffened, his focus swinging to Emma. "Yes, she's right here." He held the receiver out for her, mouthing the words, "*Your father.*"

"Dad?" Her hand clamped around the cold plastic.

"I heard about the problem last night. Two men were arrested for Derek's murder?"

"Yes."

"When were you going to tell me? I found out from a reporter contacting me for a comment."

"It's been busy around here."

"I want to see you, Emma. Can I come to Crystal Springs?"

The fact her father asked her permission robbed her of words for a few seconds. Guilt nudged her to say, "Colin and I are actually coming to Chicago. We could stop by and see you."

"When?"

"Just a moment." Emma cupped her hand over the mouthpiece and asked, "When did you want to go to Chicago?"

"Tomorrow."

"We're coming tomorrow, Dad."

"Come around noon and we can have lunch in the executive dining room. No one will bother us there."

"I'll see you then." Emma gave the receiver back to Colin to put on its base.

"You didn't tell your father you had your sight back." Grace rose.

"I suspect he already knows. He has a way of knowing things even before it's common knowledge."

"I'm going to bed. What time are y'all leaving in the morning, Colin?"

"Nine."

"Then come over for a big breakfast before you leave." Grace walked toward the door and left the room.

"She'll be all right, Emma. She's tough. The doctor said her head would hurt for a few days."

"I can't help thinking she's in pain because of me." Emma chewed on her bottom lip, hating to see Grace hurting.

"Come on. It's late. Walk me to the door." Colin offered her his hand.

She took it and he helped her to her feet. "Why couldn't either Roy or Manny confess to who they worked for and cut a deal with the D.A.? Then this would all be over with."

"And you could go on with your life."

"You, too. I imagine in the past week or so you haven't been able to do your job like you usually do."

"My congregation understands."

"From what I've seen, they're wonderful. I've never experienced anything like them. Linda brought dinner over for us tonight. She was thrilled to have been a part of those men's capture."

Colin chuckled, starting for the hallway. "When I stopped by to thank her this afternoon, she was holding court in her kitchen while she was preparing the dinner for you two. She told me everyone's prayers have changed to finding out who hired Roy and Manny now that the killers have been caught."

Emma thought about the prayer warriors, as the women of the church referred to themselves, interceding on her behalf. If they could, then she could, too. "Colin, how do you pray to God?"

At the front door, he opened it and pulled her out onto the porch. The warm spring air enveloped her with its scent of flowers and newly mowed grass. He drew her to the swing at one end and sat, tugging her down next to him.

"We haven't talked much since I gave you those tapes."

"We've been busy."

"To answer your question, Emma, my prayers are often more like conversations with the Lord. There's no right way to do it. If it comes from your heart, that's all that matters. If you or someone you know needs something, ask Him. If you want to thank Him or praise Him, just do it. There's no one way that works better than another."

Staring down at her hands laced together, she said, "When I was in the basement, I prayed to God." She peered up at him. "And He heard me. I asked for help and for Grace to be all right. But I was so afraid I didn't do it right, that my ignorance would—" She couldn't get the words past the constriction in her throat when she thought back to that feeling of terror.

"That's not important. What's important is that you asked." Colin covered her clasped hands with his.

Emotions solidified in her throat. "He heard me," she whispered again in a thick voice. "Grace is okay." Her gaze still connected to his, she licked her dry lips and continued in a strong voice, "I can't believe He answered *my* prayer."

"Why?" His grasp tightened.

"Until last Sunday I'd never gone to a church service except for weddings or funerals. I've done so many things wrong. I don't even think my parents really love me, so how can He? How can He forgive me all my sins?"

"One of my favorite verses is from the Gospel According to John. John the Baptist proclaims this when he sees Jesus coming toward him. 'Here is the Lamb of God who takes away the sins of the world!' That was why Christ walked among us, to wash away our sins. All you have to do is believe, Emma, that your Heavenly Father loves you."

She'd never really felt she belonged anywhere. The concept that God loved her unconditionally stunned her. The ice in her heart, put there from years of being alone, dissolved, and emotions flowed from her—of love toward God, of acceptance of herself as a flawed person who could be forgiven. "Is it really that simple?"

"Yes and no. All you have to do is believe in God and that His only Son died so that we could be forgiven. In Corinthians it says, 'God made Him who had no sin to be sin for us, so that in Him we might become the righteousness of God.' It doesn't get any better than that."

On overload, Emma drew her hands down her face. The emotional tangle of her feelings pushed her to her feet. She needed time to process all that had happened to her and to nurture this newfound faith budding to life within. "Thank you, Colin. This gives me a lot to think about."

Listening to the weak thread of her voice, he looked up into her glistening eyes and desperately wanted to take her into his arms and make everything crystal clear to her. But he saw her struggling to make sense of what had transpired over the past few weeks. Holding her would only complicate things. He had done what he could. Now the rest was in the hands of the Lord and Emma.

"Emma, the hard part is turning yourself totally over to the Lord, letting go of what you perceive as control over your life. Some people find it difficult to give themselves into God's hands."

"Isn't control an illusion? Do people really control their lives?" She laughed, but the sound held no humor. "I thought I did until Derek's death and everything that happened after that. I was kidding myself."

"We have free will. We have choices."

"Like my brother and how he lived his life?" Emma walked a few feet away, then swung around to face him. "I know he didn't make good choices. He made a lot of people very angry with him—enough that at least one wanted him dead. I can't ignore the information I've been discovering this past week concerning Derek. I love him, but he was…" Her voice trailed off into the silence.

"He was flawed. We all are."

"It seems to run deep in my family. My father loves to buy companies in trouble and dismantle them, not caring whose lives he's ruining. He passed that on to his son, who apparently did an excellent job, too. My mother, for a good part of her life, was America's most glamorous movie star. Only lately as she has gotten older have the roles she's taken changed, but if she could have back her youth, she would relive her life exactly the same way. She loved the idea of men everywhere drooling after her. Not your quaint, suburban family."

"I'm not sure there's such a thing." He rose and came

to her, taking her hands and yanking her toward him. "I'm not going to let anything happen to you. We're going to find out who's behind your brother's murder and your life will return to normal." He leaned toward her to feather his lips across hers.

As they kissed, her cell phone rang. After the night before, she'd decided to carry her cell phone on her. Reluctantly he pulled back while she retrieved it from her pocket and flipped it open.

"Adam! You're certainly burning the midnight oil." Emma grew tense as she listened to her accountant.

From the scowl that wiped the pleasant smile from Emma's face, Colin could tell the news wasn't good.

When she ended the call and put her phone back in her pocket, she said, "This is worse than I thought."

ELEVEN

Colin drove into the space in the underground parking garage and turned off his engine. Then he twisted around to face Emma. "After we have lunch with your dad, we'll pay your brother's partner a little visit and get some answers to the irregularities in the books."

"Irregularities? Adam thinks it's a smuggling scheme. If that's true, organized crime could be involved."

"Emma, he just said that was one possibility."

"The most likely one. What if Derek knew? What if my brother was a part of something crooked?" The very thought made Emma doubt her ability to read people at all. She'd always considered her older brother a good guy. Finding out otherwise devastated her.

"Then you'll deal with it. It's times like this when you can turn to the Lord for guidance. Emma, it's possible Derek knew nothing."

"Which means Marcus definitely had a good motive to have him killed if Derek found out and wanted to put a stop to it."

"That would move him to the top of our list, and we can let J.T. know about it. I'd like to see Marcus's reaction to you having your eyesight back. Whoever is behind the murder thinks you might be a threat."

"Then I think we should also pay Alicia a visit while we're in Chicago. She and her uncle are suspects, too."

"Then we will, after we see Marcus. This should be an interesting afternoon."

Colin opened his door and climbed out of the SUV while Emma did the same. On the elevator ride to the top floor where the executive dining room was for S&J Corporation, Emma drew in deep, calming breaths but the trembling in her hands quickly diffused throughout her body, and she clutched Colin's arm for a few seconds while the doors swished open.

A memory as a little girl with her nanny coming to see her father at work inundated her. He'd been in a meeting, too busy to see her, and she'd left that day disappointed. Not two weeks later, her mother had moved to California permanently with her. As the limousine had driven away with her and her mother for the airport, she'd looked back at the house, watching Derek alone in the driveway, waving goodbye. Her father had been nowhere around, as he had been for so much of her life.

Advancing toward the hallway that led to the dining room, Emma smiled at the receptionist she'd never seen before, then strode past her. Emma ignored the woman trying to stop her and entered the spacious room with eight tables set with white linens, bone china and crystal. The silver gleamed in the noonday sun that streamed in through the large floor-to-ceiling windows that afforded a million-dollar view of Lake Michigan and Chicago.

Emma came to a stop a few feet in. Her father stood

by a window and turned as the door opened behind Emma. He smiled.

"Sir, I'm sorry about—" the young receptionist said.

William St. James waved his hand. "That's okay, Gloria. This is my daughter."

Pride wove its way through his words. The warmth in her father's expression rested on Emma, causing hope to plant itself deep in her heart. Did he truly care? Then she remembered the years he had been absent from her life and decided she was dreaming to think that.

The sound of the door closing shut the rest of the world out. The only people in the room were her, Colin slightly to the left of her and her father ten feet in front. Silence ruled for a long, uncomfortable moment while Emma resisted the urge to squirm. Her father was the master of the intimidating look, and she was determined not to let it get to her.

"When were you going to tell me you got your sight back?" Her father's bushy eyebrows beetled together.

"I figured you already knew. You're so resourceful, there's little you don't know." She lifted her chin a notch. "It happened when those men tried to kill me."

The frown on his face eased but only slightly as he gestured toward a table near him. "Sit. Charles will take your drink order." He nodded toward a small man who had entered the dining room from the kitchen.

Colin held out the chair for her, then scooted it toward the table before taking his seat next to hers. He gave her a reassuring smile, which bolstered her confidence. She'd need it in dealing with her father. After giving Charles their order, Emma opened her napkin and smoothed it in her lap while trying to decide what to say next.

Her father broke the silence with, "You could have been killed the other night, Emma."

For a brief moment she thought she'd heard a wobble in her father's voice, but she had to be mistaken. That would mean he cared what happened to her. Her whole life, all she'd ever wanted from him was an indication he loved her. "I wasn't," she finally said, studying the neutral expression on his face. He'd always been so good at concealing his emotions, to the point she didn't know what her father felt.

"I want—" William St. James paused while Charles placed their iced teas on the table, then waited until the man left again before continuing. "I want you to come stay with me until this whole affair is settled. Next time you might not be so lucky."

The strength in her father's voice faded until she barely heard the last word. When her eyes drilled into his, he averted his glance toward the door into the kitchen. "Dad?" A wealth of questions lay in that one word.

After coughing several times, William called out, "Charles, we'll order lunch now." Then to them he said, "The prime rib is wonderful," as though this was an everyday occurrence and the atmosphere didn't pulsate with tension.

Again Charles came out and took down what they wanted to eat, then disappeared into the kitchen. Once more, silence electrified the air as if a storm brewed. Emma contemplated the dark look in her father's eyes. *Did* he care? she wondered and again dismissed that notion as not possible.

"I can secure my estate tighter than an oil drum. Will you come to Chicago, Emma?" Her father took a sip of his drink, watching her over the rim of his glass.

His estate, the one she'd left over twenty years ago. The place where her last image was of Derek alone on the driveway, the only one to say goodbye. She wouldn't, *couldn't* go back there. She looked toward Colin, gathering the strength she needed to face her father. "No. I can't."

"Why not?"

She didn't know how to explain all the feelings tangled up inside her—the confusion, the sadness, the uncertainty in her life, the budding love she felt toward Colin, the need to commit herself to the Lord, something her father would never understand. He would never turn control of his life over to another. "I'm safe where I am," was all she could say, which was enough by the thunderous expression that descended on her father's face.

"Safe? You were hunted down and almost killed there! I don't call that safe. What's changed? You have bodyguards now?"

"No. We're close to discovering who was behind Derek's murder. The two men who shot him are in jail. I would say the situation is vastly improved."

"Nothing has changed! The man responsible is still out there. He sent those goons to kill you!" Her father bent forward, his fists resting on the table.

"Why? I can't identify him, only the two men. That's why they came after me."

"Maybe."

Her father's doubt manifested itself in her, and she

began to wonder about the attempt on her life. Was there more to it? Did she know something she wasn't remembering? Were they close to discovering the person behind her brother's murder?

"Dad, I didn't come here to argue with you. I'm staying in Crystal Springs for the time being." She put a forcefulness behind her words, hoping her father would let the subject drop.

As though everything was fine, he straightened his silverware next to his plate as Charles came into the room with their lunch. "Then you won't mind me having my own private detectives looking into Derek's murder."

"I'm surprised you haven't already," Emma said as the waiter placed her prime rib with vegetables and scalloped potatoes in front of her. Although the aromas teased her senses with thoughts of the mouthwatering food, the idea of eating clenched her stomach.

Her father waited until Charles left before saying, "Actually, I have."

Colin took a sip from his iced tea. "Have they found out anything?"

"Have you?"

Colin glanced at Emma, and she nodded. They needed all the assistance they could get, and if pooling resources helped, then she was all for it.

"We have a list of people we're checking into." Colin cut into his prime rib. "There's Marcus Peterson."

"I never did want Derek to partner with him. I don't like the man's methods."

She nearly choked on her meat. "His methods?"

Her father's sharp eyes settled on her. "I told Derek a few weeks ago that his partner is living above his means and that he has an expensive gambling habit. Derek wasn't aware of that."

"Do you think your son did some investigating and discovered something was going on?"

"Knowing Derek, yes." Shifting his attention back to Colin, William scowled. "Is he your prime suspect?"

"Emma found out last night from her accountant that the books don't add up. Something's wrong with the business. We think he's funneling stolen goods through it. We're going to the office when we leave here to see what Marcus has to say for himself."

"Do you think that's wise?"

"If he had Derek killed, we're putting him on notice. The irregularities in the company books will be investigated no matter what. Having something happen to Emma won't change that. That will be made clear from the beginning. Besides, there'll be a lot of people around in the middle of the afternoon."

The barely leashed control in Colin's voice brought back memories of how well he had taken care of the two men several nights ago, reinforcing in her mind that he was a man of contradictions—gentle and tough, a man of God and a warrior.

"I hope so, for my daughter's sake."

Emma heard again the concern in her father's words. She eyed him and for a brief moment thought she saw worry in his expression before his usual mask fell into place.

"Sir, I'll do everything in my power to make sure nothing happens to Emma. You have my word."

Colin's steady regard, coupled with the fierceness in his tone, underscored his intent to keep her safe.

Knowing that warmed her insides, easing whatever trepidation she had in seeing Marcus, face-to-face.

Surprisingly her father broke visual contact with Colin, saying, "Do you suspect anyone else?"

"There's always Jerry Lunsford and Alexander Sims. For that matter, anyone else Derek bankrupted in the past few years. You would know better than us who that might be. After all, he worked for you." Emma's grip tightened on her fork as she brought it to her mouth.

The hard line of her father's jaw clenched and his eyes narrowed. "I'm not going to argue with you over my business practices. They're all legal."

"Legal doesn't always mean right."

"I have provided jobs for thousands."

"And you have put thousands out of work by shutting down companies and plants. Any of those people could be holding a grudge against Derek. Our list might not even include the man behind my brother's murder."

Her father grasped the edge of the table, anger carved into his face. "If they aren't profitable, then they shouldn't be in business."

"Ah, yes. The strongest survive." She speared some glazed carrots and popped them into her mouth, not because she was hungry but because she needed to do something.

"Yes. That's business."

Emma chewed her vegetables, but she couldn't taste their sweetness. With a parched throat, she took a large swallow of her tea. She ignored her father's glare and asked, "Is there anyone else beside Alexander Sims and Jerry Lunsford that Derek was instrumental in ruining?"

Her father shot to his feet, tossing his napkin onto the

table. "Your brother didn't ruin those men. They did it all by themselves. We were there to pick up the pieces and salvage what we could of their companies."

Emma stood, facing her father across the small table for four. "Are there any more?"

"I don't know. I suppose there might be." His voice rose with each word, a defensiveness she'd never heard in it.

"Then I suggest you find out. What Derek did for you could have been the reason he was killed."

The second she said what she had been thinking for over a week, she regretted the outburst. The look of pain that flashed into her father's eyes tore at her defenses. For a few seconds she saw the hurt she had caused and wished she hadn't said anything even though it might be the truth.

Her father pivoted away from the table and strode to the bank of windows. The rigid set of his body contradicted the slight trembling she glimpsed in his hands, which he immediately stuffed into the pockets of his black suit.

Colin came up to her side and whispered, "I think I need to leave you two alone for a few minutes. Talk to him, Emma. He needs it and so do you."

He started toward the door. Emma grabbed for him, not wanting to be alone with her father. Her fingers brushed across his back, then Colin was out of her reach and striding toward the exit.

The door clicking shut made her flinch as though she had been hit. She turned back to her father, at a loss for words. After her parents' divorce, he hadn't been in her life much. Even the occasional visit with him had been strained, as if all they had in common was the same last name—and their love for Derek. That thought made Emma take a step toward her father. Then another.

"Dad? I'm sorry. I shouldn't have said that."

His shoulders sagged as though he carried an unseen burden on them. "But you meant every word."

She wanted to deny it, but she wouldn't lie. Instead, she came closer until she stood next to him at the window and stared at the city below with the glittering lake in the background. "I've discovered Derek made a few enemies. It was hard for me to reconcile the Derek I'm hearing about with the Derek I knew and loved as my brother."

"I made him that way. Isn't that what you really want to say? He was becoming like me?"

"Yes." The dryness in her mouth prevented her from saying any more than that.

"I know this past year or so Derek and I had our misunderstandings, but we did respect and care for each other. I knew almost from the beginning my son didn't really have what it took to be ruthless and cutthroat in the business world. He stuck it out for as long as he could because he hadn't wanted to disappoint me."

She and her brother had wanted the same thing and neither one had succeeded. "Why does the bottom line always have to be about money?"

"I head a large corporation. I have responsibilities to the shareholders and to the people who depend on S&J Corporation for a job. Making money is what business is all about."

"How about your responsibilities to your family?"

Silence greeted that question.

What was she doing here trying to understand her

father? Did she think she could make a bid for his love now after all these years? Being around Colin had made her think anything was possible—even her father's love. She took a step back, aware of the silence lengthening, her nerves stretched taut.

Her father's shoulders hunched even more. He stared down at the street below. "Don't you understand, Emma, my company is the only place where I have been successful? I wasn't a good husband and I certainly wasn't a good father, not to Derek and especially not to you." He twisted around, a desolate look on his face. "It's not easy for me to admit failure. Most people would think my life was hugely successful." His laugh held self-mockery. "But you and I know the real truth. Derek did. Even your mother does. I'm lousy at relationships. I drove her into the arms of another man. My parents never loved me, could only tolerate me around for a very short time. I grew up in one boarding school after another. I don't know how to love."

Shocked by his admission, Emma stepped back another foot. Words failed her.

"Our relationship is so bad you would rather stay with a stranger than me even though your life may be in danger. That, above all else, speaks louder than anything you could ever say to me."

Her heart bled as if he had taken a knife and thrust it into her. Again she wanted to deny the words but couldn't. He was right about her reasons for staying in Crystal Springs—at least, at the beginning. Not now. Now she wanted to stay because…because she was in love with Colin, a man from a different world than hers, a man whose life revolved around God and his family.

"How do I repair the damage I've done to us?"

Her father's question brought tears to her eyes. *You could start by telling me you love me.* She wanted to say those words, but they couldn't get past the lump in her throat. She closed her eyes and drew in a deep breath, then another.

"I'm not good at—" Her father's voice came to a halt.

Emma opened her eyes and saw the anguish and struggle playing across his features. "Good at what?"

"At expressing my—" another long pause while he visibly swallowed "—my feelings."

"What are they?" she asked in a whisper, her voice roughened with the tears she was trying to hold back.

"You are my daughter."

"I know, but what does that mean to you?" *I can't read your mind!*

He turned back to the window, silence falling again.

"Dad?" She advanced toward him, realizing she had to make the first move. In the past, her pride would have kept her rooted where she was, her emotions locked up inside her. But remembering Jesus' words about forgiveness, she couldn't. "All I've ever wanted from you is your love." She placed her hand on his arm. "I love you, Dad." She might not like the things her father had done, but she had always loved him, had wanted to be accepted by him, had lashed out when she didn't think she was.

He covered her hand, his grip tight. "I've lost my son. No parent should ever have to go through watching… their child…being buried." With his voice raw as if it were an open wound, he cleared his throat, paused a few seconds, then shifted toward her, bleakness dulling his blue eyes. "I don't want to lose you, Emma. You're too important to me."

She *really* embraced her father for the first time. He hadn't told her he loved her, but it was a start that she knew he cared for her. "You won't. I promise."

He drew back. "How can you make that promise?"

He is my refuge and my fortress; My God, in Him I will trust. Feeling as though she wasn't alone, that God walked with her, she said, "I just can. No matter what happens you have my love. And when this is over with, we can start fresh as father and daughter—if you want."

"You could always relocate to Chicago. Your job doesn't require you to live in New York."

In the past his controlling habit would have irritated her, but it didn't now. Emma shook her head, laughing. "You'll never change."

He grinned. "Probably not."

"Chicago and New York aren't too far apart. A few hours by plane. We'll make it work."

"I guess we should bring in your young man before he thinks we've fallen off the face of the earth."

Your young man. Although her feelings for Colin were deep, there was so much going on in her life that she couldn't see a future for them. How could she expect what she was experiencing to last when her life was changing every minute that passed? "He's a friend, Dad. That's all," she finally said as her father ambled across the dining room.

He stopped at the door and glanced back at her. "That's not how it appears to me. Something's going on between you two that has nothing to do with finding the person behind Derek's murder. I've checked into Colin

Fitzpatrick. He isn't someone I would have picked for you, but he's a good man."

Before Emma could reply to her father's casual comment about investigating Colin, he opened the door and motioned for Colin to come back into the room. When she thought about it, she realized she shouldn't be surprised, knowing how her father operated. In fact, she should be flattered he'd cared enough to check up on Colin.

As he entered, Emma noticed Brandon right behind him. He'd said he was coming to Chicago on business, but she hadn't realized that business was with her father.

Pleasantly surprised, she made her way to Brandon and hugged him, his grasp on her tight as he pressed her close. "It's nice to see you."

Stunned, Brandon pulled back. "You can see! When did that happen?"

"A few nights ago. What brings you here?"

"I told you I was coming to Chicago."

Dismissing the edge to Brandon's voice, Emma chuckled. "I meant *here*." She pointed to the floor.

He blinked, then smiled. "Oh, I have business with your father. I'm glad I came a little early or I would have missed your visit and the good news." His grin grew to encompass his whole face. "How did you get your eyesight back?"

As Emma retold what had happened the night the two men tried to kill her, she realized she would probably be telling the story a lot over the next few days.

"But you weren't hurt?" Brandon asked, concern in his eyes.

"No. On the contrary, I'm regaining my memory by leaps and bounds."

"Good." Brandon flicked a glance toward Colin. "When you return to New York, we'll have to go out to dinner and celebrate your recovery."

Her father moved forward. "Right now, Emma and her young man have business across town."

She looked at her father, the air chilly. There were those words "her young man" again. What was up with him? Was it possible that her father was giving Colin his stamp of approval and also letting Brandon know that? The very idea was intriguing and novel, putting a bounce in Emma's walk as she left the floor.

"This place looks deserted." Emma went through one of the double glass doors that Colin held open for her that led into the corporate offices of East West Imports.

No one sat behind the reception desk. The lights were off except for one in an office at the end of the corridor, its door agape. The eerie quiet sent a shiver down Emma, causing her steps to falter.

Colin came up behind her and whispered, "Let's check out that office." He pointed toward the stream of light coming from the partially opened door.

A phone rang at the reception desk. Emma jumped, holding in a gasp, her heart thudding against her chest. Placing her hand over it, she breathed deeply while the insistent ringing continued. Blissfully halfway down the corridor the disturbing sound ceased, and the rapid beat of her heart slowed a little.

From her visit a year ago when the company first opened, she knew that office was Marcus's. Were they going to be confronting her brother's killer? Maybe this wasn't such a good idea, she thought, when she glanced about at the deserted place. Where were the people who were supposed to be working? They were to be their insurance.

Emma paused three-fourths of the way to the office and leaned close to Colin. "Let's let the police handle this. I don't—"

The stream of light became a flood as Marcus nudged the door open with his foot because his hands were full carrying a large box. He froze when he saw them, the carton slipping from his grasp.

Its crash echoed down the lonely corridor.

Emma gulped, inching closer to Colin.

Taking her hand, Colin strode forward. "We need to have a few words with you."

Marcus rushed toward them.

TWELVE

In the hallway of East West Imports corporate offices, Emma stood her ground as Marcus charged them. But instead of attacking, the tall, slightly overweight man plowed by both Colin and her, heading for the elevator.

"Hold it!" Emma yelled, whirling around. "You can't leave. We have business to discuss."

Marcus threw her a wild-eyed glance before barreling through the double glass doors. He skidded to a halt at the elevators and punched the down button. Tapping his foot, he waited, avoiding looking at them, as though that would make them go away.

"He isn't gonna make this easy," Colin muttered, and raced toward Marcus.

Derek's partner spun on his heel, then dashed for the stairs at the other end of the corridor. Colin caught up with him as the man wrenched open the door leading down to the ground floor.

While Emma ran toward the pair, Colin pinned Marcus against the wall with his forearm, his larger, more muscular body blocking the man's escape. Guilt was written all over Marcus's face. This had been Derek's partner and friend. And yet, he'd betrayed her brother. She had every intention of discovering how deep that betrayal was before she left today. Anger festered inside, and Emma had to stop a few feet from them to gather her composure before saying anything.

Marcus locked stares with her, his jaw twitching. "You can see!"

Was that panic she'd heard in his voice? She continued to glare at him, and he looked away.

"I'm going to release you, but don't try to run."

The menace in Colin's voice would have rooted her to the spot. Thankfully, as he backed away from Marcus, the heavyset man took Colin's advice. Marcus pressed himself against the wall, his body rigid as an ice statue. He wouldn't look at her but kept his focus trained on Colin.

"Why were you leaving?" Emma asked, coming up to stand next to Colin, hoping to force Marcus to acknowledge her presence.

The man clamped his jaws so tightly she again saw a nerve jump in his cheek.

"Were you packing up? Going somewhere?" Emma gestured in the direction of the double doors that led into the East West Imports offices.

"I don't have to say anything to you."

"I'm Derek's beneficiary, as well as the executor of his estate. Since I'm now your new partner, I think I have a right to know what's going on."

"Then it seems to me you gain the most from your brother's death," Marcus said, turning his attention, full of contempt, on her.

His accusation stunned her. It shouldn't have, because people had been murdered for that very reason, but it did. Hurt mingled with the anger growing rapidly inside her. She squeezed between him and Colin, lifting her chin so she wouldn't miss a fleeting expression on the man's face.

"The person who has a good motive for killing Derek is you. There'll be a full investigation of this company, and what you've been doing will be uncovered. Things don't add up. I have a feeling my brother found out and that's why he was murdered."

Before she realized what Marcus intended, he shoved her into Colin, sending them both to the carpeted floor. Marcus flew past them through the double doors and toward his office. He disappeared inside as Emma scrambled to her feet and started after the man, not wanting him to get away when he could be responsible for her brother's death. Inside the darkened offices, Emma headed toward Marcus's at the end of the hallway.

Colin grabbed her arm, stopping her. "Let's get out of here and call the police. Something's definitely wrong."

"Yeah, he had my brother killed." Anger still drove her forward.

Colin held her, finally stilling her movements completely. "Emma, I promised your dad nothing would happen to you, and I intend to keep that promise."

Panting, she stopped her struggle to get free and twisted back toward Colin. Seeing reason in his expression calmed the rage boiling in her.

He raised his hands and cupped her face. "It's not worth it if you get hurt."

"I know." The feel of his palms against her skin warmed the coldness that had gripped her since seeing Marcus. Colin's caring concern soothed her pain. "Let's leave and call from the lobby."

"You aren't calling anyone," came Marcus's voice from the doorway into his office.

Emma swung around and saw the gun in his hand. Then she noticed something else—the almost desperate, wild look in Marcus's eyes was taking over his whole expression.

He intended to kill them!

She backed away and came up flat against Colin. "Marcus, put that gun down."

"No," he shouted, waving it in front of him. "I'm leaving the country today and you two aren't stopping me. If I don't, they'll kill me. Get in here." Stepping from the entrance, he motioned with the weapon for them to go into his office.

Her whole body quaking, Emma walked toward Marcus. "Who are they?"

"The people I owe money to. If Derek hadn't started snooping around, I could have repaid them and no one would have been the wiser. I just had a couple more shipments and I would have been home-free. But no, your brother had to stick his nose into my business and now you have, too."

At the door Emma squared off. "So you killed him… over money?"

Marcus's bushy eyebrows slashed downward. "I didn't kill him."

"Hiring someone to kill him is the same as doing it yourself."

Marcus flinched as if she'd slapped him. "I don't know who killed Derek. I'd have come up with another way to get the money given time, but I don't have that time anymore with everything going on. My…creditors are getting impatient. I can't stay here any longer. They want their money. *Now*." He thrust his face close to hers. "Because of *you*."

Colin made a move toward him.

Marcus leaped back. "Get inside before I use this gun. I abhor violence, but I'll use it if I have to."

If their situation wasn't so dire, she would have laughed at Marcus's last statement. Instead, she did as she was told and entered the office, the place in a shambles. "This is a mess. You need to hire better cleaning people."

"This is the way I found it. It's a message I'm not taking lightly." Again he used the gun to point toward a closet along a wall behind his desk. "You two get in there. I just need a few hours then everything will be all right."

Moving toward the closet, Emma glanced back at Marcus. Sweat beaded his forehead and his hand with the gun quaked. He'd loosened his tie and his hair looked as though he'd run his fingers through it over and over. It wasn't guilt she had seen earlier but fear in his expression.

"The cleaning people show up after-hours. You shouldn't be in here too long. You go in first," Marcus said to Colin. When Colin was inside and turned to face Marcus, the heavyset man said, "Turn your pockets inside out. I want to make sure you don't have a cell phone."

After satisfying himself that Colin didn't have one, Marcus shifted his attention to Emma. "You're next." He stripped her purse from her shoulder and snapped it open. While keeping his attention on them, he felt around in her bag until he found her cell phone. He took it and tossed her purse into the closet. "Get in."

When Emma came to the doorway of what looked more like a large storage area than a coat closet, Marcus pushed her inside and slammed the door. The lock clicked. She tried the handle. It wouldn't budge. They were trapped in the closet, in the dark. Before the accident, terror would have seized her immediately. The dark had always frightened her. Not now. Its velvet blackness placated her. At least, they were alive.

Through the door she heard Marcus say, "I just need a few hours, then I'll be safe." She thought he repeated that sentence again, but the words were muffled so she wasn't sure.

She banged on the door and yelled, "Let us out!" more out of frustration than the hope that it would help. The office was deserted and Marcus Peterson was going to get away, probably leave the country as he had said earlier.

"You okay?" Colin asked, his hand brushing against her arm.

"Fine. But my brother's murderer is getting away."

"I don't think he did it."

"You don't?" His touch reassured her that everything would be all right. His fresh scent, which reminded her of the outdoors, wafted to her and further relaxed some of her frustration and desperation that Marcus was going to get away.

"No, just a gut feeling. From what he admitted, he was definitely using the company to pay off his gambling debts, but I don't think he had your brother killed."

After searching the area by the door, Emma sagged against the wall, fingering the shelving next to her. "Where's a light switch when you need it?"

"I saw it on the outside."

"I guess we have to wait until the cleaning people arrive." She heard Colin rummaging around in the dark and asked, "What are you looking for?"

"Something heavy to use against the door. They're usually hollow so I might be able to break through."

Emma joined him in the search of the large closet's contents, finding mostly boxes with papers in them. As the minutes ticked by and nothing seemed to fit what Colin needed, her spirits began to wane. She didn't want Marcus to get away. She wasn't totally convinced he hadn't had her brother murdered.

Please, Lord, help us get out of here!

Five minutes later Colin said, "I found something. It's a desk lamp. I think I can use its body as a hammer. Stand back in the corner." He pushed her gently away.

The sounds of the metal hitting the wood reverberated through the closet, loud, crashing. Over and over, Colin struck the door until streams of light from the office broke through, illuminating the dark. Finally he had a big enough hole in the wood to stick his hand through and unlock the door with the key that Marcus had left in it.

When Colin opened it, allowing fresh air to rush in, Emma breathed deeply and thanked God for His help. More and more she was realizing her first instinct was to turn to the Lord for help or guidance. That reinforced the feeling she wasn't alone anymore.

"I'm glad Marcus was nice enough to leave the key. Probably so the cleaning people could get us out. That's one of the reasons I don't think he was involved in murder. He could have killed us instead of locking us in the closet."

"Maybe," Emma murmured, not sure what to think.

In the office Colin went to the phone and called J.T. and told him everything that had happened. "He's probably at the airport."

When Colin hung up, he faced Emma. "Madison was there and she's calling the Chicago police. They'll pick up Marcus, hopefully before he gets a chance to leave Chicago. We'll need to file a complaint against him."

She eased back against the desk. "Derek trusted Marcus and look what he did to my brother."

"As I said, I'm not convinced he had your brother killed."

"I know. Even if he didn't, he was robbing my brother and using the company for illegal activities just to satisfy his gambling debts."

"Desperate people do desperate things. I still want to go see Alicia Harris. Are you up for it after we finish at the police station?"

"Sure. Why not? I would love to know why she was seeing my brother. It couldn't have been because she loved him as she claimed at the funeral."

"Once she realizes you know who she is I'm sure she'll enlighten us," Colin said, making his way toward the elevator.

"And it won't be flattering."

The doors opened and Colin stepped onto the elevator. "It won't be easy to hear. Will you be okay?"

"Truthfully, no, but it's something that needs to be done. My picture of Derek is so different from others. That's not to say mine isn't wrong. He was a good brother. What I'm discovering about Derek won't change that. I'd always thought my older brother could do no wrong. I'm finding out he could and did. As you pointed out before, no one is perfect, and he deserves forgiveness, too."

An hour and a half later Colin found a parking space across the street from the three-story red brick building that housed Alicia Harris's design center.

Emma hastened across the street and paused outside From Top to Bottom Designs. She waited for him before entering.

Inside the brightly lit studio a couple sat looking through some wallpaper books while one of Alicia's assistants helped them. Alicia was on the phone and looked up when he and Emma came in. The smile of greeting died on the beautiful woman's face for a few seconds before she turned away. She said a few words to the person on the other end then hung up. Quickly she headed toward them, her smile in full force.

"Emma. I didn't expect you. What brings you by?"

"I wanted to have a few words with you in private." Emma glanced at the couple and the assistant at the table along the far wall.

"You've gotten your sight back! That's wonderful!"

The woman's voice held a false ring to it that made Emma stiffen beside him. Colin took her hand within his and squeezed gently, a connection instantly flowing between them, something that still amazed him—this bond he had with Emma. And she continued to astonish him with how well she was holding up with all that she had endured the past few weeks. Emma reminded him of Grace in a lot of ways—a determined fighter.

"Can we talk in your office?" Emma asked, striding toward a door at the back.

"Well, yes, I suppose." Alicia hurried in front of them and opened the door, entering her office first. "Is something wrong?"

"Why would anything be wrong?" Emma prowled around the room as though she could barely contain her energy.

"This is most unusual. You've never visited here before."

"Because I live in New York. If I'd lived here, I might have noticed something wasn't quite right with your motive for dating my brother."

Alicia drew herself up, squaring her shoulders. "I beg your pardon?"

"Let me put it another way. Why would Alexander Sims's favorite niece date Derek St. James, the man her uncle declared ruined him?"

The silence was deafening in its intensity. In the car on the way over here, Emma had wanted him to watch Alicia and her reactions for any sign that might indicate her involvement in Derek's death. What he saw on the woman's face at that moment was lingering hatred revealed after months of keeping it hidden.

"So you know." Alicia sank onto her tan leather chair behind her desk and relaxed back, elbows resting on the arms of the chair while she steepled her fingers. "I'm glad I don't have to pretend to love your brother anymore. It was taxing my nerves."

Emma opened her mouth then snapped it closed, her hand holding his crushing him. Finally she asked, "Why did you do it?"

"Simple. To find his weak spot for my uncle. But I'd come to the conclusion your brother was as cold and ruthless as your father." Alicia scooted her chair closer to the desk and picked up a pen. "Now if you will excuse me, I've got work to do."

"Did you have him killed because you couldn't find a way to ruin him?"

The question dangled in the air between Emma and Alicia. Alicia lifted her head and stabbed Emma with a cold glare.

"What do you expect?" Alicia finally asked. "A confession? Death was too easy for Derek. So no, I didn't have him killed. I would have done it myself if I'd wanted him dead. My uncle raised me and was a wonderful, kind man who changed after your family got through with him."

Emma took a step toward Alicia. Colin swung around in front of Emma and whispered, "We got what we came for."

Emma nodded. At the door, she paused and glanced back at Alicia. "You really aren't very smart. The papa rattler is still alive and well."

Outside, the sun had disappeared behind the tall buildings to the west. The warm, humid air stuck to Colin. A breeze ruffled the yellow awning on the store next to the design studio. People crowded the sidewalk, all heading home for dinner.

"Let's get back to Crystal Springs. I've had enough of the big city." Colin unlocked his SUV for Emma, then rounded the front and slid in behind the steering wheel. "We can talk on the way home."

Home. Emma liked the sound of that word. Her apartment in New York had never really conjured the image of home in her mind; it was just a place to eat and sleep. But Crystal Springs felt like home. That thought sent panic zipping through her. She had it far worse than she'd realized.

When Colin was outside of Chicago, Emma said, "We should go back to the cabin."

"It's messier than Marcus's office. Are you sure?"

"Yes. I need to remember something but I can't. Maybe going back to the scene of the crime will jog my memory. It helped last time."

"And it also left you emotionally devastated."

"Our visits to Alicia and Marcus didn't produce the killer or any leads to the evidence we need. I'm still not convinced one of them isn't responsible. I've *got* to do something."

"Then we'll go first thing in the morning."

The prospects of seeing the cabin again chilled Emma, but she had to do it. She couldn't shake the feeling she held the key to this whole mystery locked inside her subconscious mind.

Colin turned onto the road leading to the cabin. "J.T. is traveling to Chicago to have a few words with Marcus. They found him at the airport about to board a plane for Brazil. The police won't be able to hold him long. J.T. doesn't think the kidnapping charges will stick."

"I didn't think they would when we gave our statement yesterday, but if it'll keep Marcus in the country for an extra day, great."

"I don't believe he's behind your brother's murder,

but I think the people he owes money to will be keeping an eye on him. I doubt he'll be going anywhere. It'll give us time to straighten things out."

Emma tensed as she glimpsed the family log cabin through the trees. The place had held such wonderful memories of her childhood spent at the lake—a time before her mother was so famous she couldn't go anywhere and not be recognized, before her father had turned his family's failing company into a power to be reckoned with, before her mother left her ten-year marriage. But now all she'd ever be able to think about was the last time she'd seen Derek.

"Confronting Marcus was the only good thing that came out of yesterday's trip to Chicago."

Colin came to a stop in front of the cabin and twisted around to face her. "I thought you and your dad had a good talk."

"Well, yes. I meant concerning Derek."

"You haven't said too much about what went on with your dad. Do you want to talk about it?"

Until Colin, Emma had never shared her feelings with anyone except her brother. She didn't have a lot of close friends. She had told herself the reason was because she traveled so much in her job. But the real truth was she had never trusted anyone enough to expose her inner thoughts. She'd been used by too many others in the past who had wanted to get close to one of her parents not to question people's motives for wanting to be her friend. That she trusted Colin only emphasized how much he meant to her and also the kind of power he held over her.

"Dad and I came to an understanding of sorts. At

least, I hope so. For years he was this distant person who was my father but also a stranger. I hope that'll change in the future. I told him I would visit him and hoped that he would come see me in New York." She offered Colin a grin. "Of course, he did his best to try and get me to move to Chicago. I told him no. New York is—where I live." She had started to say New York was her home, but she couldn't voice those words because she now knew it wasn't really a home to her, just a place she lived.

"Could you ever consider living somewhere else?"

Colin's question produced visions of Crystal Springs, laughter, family, companionship and love, bound together by a strong faith in God. But also it brought forth her fear that she would never fit in, that she was too different to be happy in a small town, that any feelings that had developed the past few weeks weren't real because of the intense, unusual circumstances. "I don't know," she answered honestly, the only way she could. "So much has changed in my life. To say I've been overwhelmed is an understatement."

His mouth curved upward, his eyes warm. "I can understand that. A lot *has* happened." He placed his hand on the handle. "Are you ready?"

Taking a calming breath, Emma pushed open her door. "About as ready as I ever will be."

Standing, facing the cabin, Emma waited until Colin came around his SUV before heading toward the porch. Her heart thundered in her ears, drowning out the sounds of the birds and insects. Its pulsating beat increased as she neared the front door. With trembling hands, she reached for the handle. Colin did so at the same time and his fingers covered hers.

"You set the pace, Emma. I'm here as an observer and to help if you need it." He slipped his hand away.

Missing his touch, she nodded and shoved the door open. She crossed the threshold. The mess before her snatched her breath, holding it trapped in her lungs until it hurt. She blew out the stale air, her gaze traveling around the main room.

"They really did search everything. What would they have been looking for?"

"That's the question we need to answer," Colin said, laying his hands on her shoulders and kneading them.

She wanted to spin around and bury herself against his solid strength. She wanted to give in to the wonderful feel of his fingers as they massaged her tension away. She wanted to erase the past two weeks. But most of all she wanted the person behind her brother's murder to be caught and stand trial. And that wouldn't happen if she didn't remember *everything*.

"Let's go through this room then the bedroom. Maybe something will trigger my memory." Emma started forward, the sound of her footsteps muffled by the indoor/outdoor carpet.

As she rummaged through the chaos, she saw nothing that made her think anything beyond how hopeless the task seemed. She was nearly complete with her examination of the main room when she spied a photo album in the corner. Because there wasn't anywhere to sit, she sank down onto the floor and scooped up the pieces of the album. Although the pictures were intact, they were scattered all about.

Fingering the leather covering, she remembered this album as a child. There was a photo of her mother, gorgeous and beautifully dressed, posing for the camera as she always did. She used to laugh about the cabin being her rustic retreat, even strangely enjoyed getting away from it all. Another was of her and Derek standing by the well with huge Cheshire cat grins on their faces. A third picture showed the whole family sitting around a picnic table outside the cabin. It appeared for the camera as if they were having a wonderful time. She remembered that had been their last outing as a family. The following week her parents had separated.

Touching the photo, she wondered what had happened. She often thought *she* had done something wrong to cause her parents to divorce. Now she knew that wasn't true, but she still wondered how much people really cherished marriage. Was that why she'd never married? Her mother had had four husbands through the years while her father hadn't remarried but had dated multiple ladies, often making the society pages with a new, younger woman on his arm, as though always searching for something elusive, just out of his reach. She didn't want to end up like either parent, but what kind of foundation did she have for a lasting relationship?

"Find anything?"

"No, just memories." Emma put the photo album on a table that Colin had righted. She would take it with her and put the pictures into a new album and relish the connection to a past she had spent years trying to forget.

"Let's check the bedroom."

She followed Colin into the smaller room, not encouraged by what had happened so far. Not one spark. Nothing. Nada.

She walked to the closet to start there. When she opened the door, a jumbled mess accosted her. Every article of Derek's clothing was tossed on the floor, boxes on the upper shelves emptied and their contents thrown everywhere. Her shoulders sagged at the sight. Dismayed, she leaned into the jamb.

"Forget what happened here. Concentrate on remembering," Colin said right behind her.

"With everything torn apart, we're probably missing something important."

A noise behind Emma brought her around. The door to the bedroom slammed shut. "Colin!"

He was already racing toward the door. He pushed on it, but it held firm. "Must be something up against the door. There'll be no busting our way out this time. This door is solid wood."

"Only the best for a St. James cabin," Emma said, hearing a hysterical ring to her words. Quickly she tamped down her fear. It wouldn't do her any good. "Why did someone lock us in here?"

Colin sniffed the air. "I've got an awful feeling about this. Is that smoke?"

Emma inhaled deeply and the scent of smoke filled her nostrils, fear returning to pump adrenaline and blood rapidly through her system. She scanned for another way out of the room. The only window was high and narrow—too narrow for her to fit through. Trapped with no way out but through a blocked door.

She reached into her pocket where she kept her cell

phone and came up empty. Marcus had taken hers yesterday. Colin had his, but it was in his SUV.

Whiffs of smoke oozed under the door, saturating the air with its deadly smell. If they made it out of the bedroom, they might still be trapped. Quickly she took some clothing and stuffed it under the door, coughing as she inhaled the smoke. Even if they had been able to place a call, help wouldn't get here in time.

Lord, I need You! Please help us get out. Don't leave us. Please, Lord, hear my prayer.

After doing his own survey of the room, Colin said, "This is the only way out so I've got to move whatever is blocking the door."

He plastered his body against the wood and shoved against it. The muscles in his arms bunched from the strain. Sweat popped out on his forehead and rolled down his face.

The door gave an inch. More smoke seeped through the crack.

While Colin rammed his body continually against the wooden barrier, Emma looked around for something to cover their faces with. If only they had water to douse a cloth down. They would have to make do with what they had.

Finally, with shirts covering their faces, Emma joined Colin, using her body as a battering ram, too. The air in the bedroom became hazy, the stinging smell churning her stomach, a series of coughs racking her even though she had a shirt wrapped around her face.

Lord, we need You.

Her shoulder ached but slowly the crack widened until she heard, over the noise of the fire, a chair fall.

Peering into the main room, through the heavy smoke, Emma saw bright yellow-orange flames shooting up the walls of the cabin, eating their way toward them. The fire's roar crackled in the air, the sounds growing louder.

"We don't have much of a choice, Emma. Crouch down low with this around your mouth and nose and head for the door. Don't breathe unless you have to." Colin secured the blue polo shirt that had loosened around his face and started forward, skirting the fallen chair and cabinet that had been used to block their escape.

Coughing, the acrid scent choking her, she covered her mouth and nose with not only the shirt but her hand, too, and followed right behind Colin. Low running, he zigzagged through the maze of flames and smoke. The stench bled through the cotton, prodding her forward faster. The heat blasted her from all sides.

Colin stopped. Before them, the blaze consumed the front door.

Blocked. Trapped.

Quickly he altered his path and headed toward a large window. Near it, he took a chair and threw it at the glass. It shattered, leaving a hole that looked as if it were a gaping mouth with fangs. The rush of oxygen into the room fed the fire, which suddenly expanded with a new energy. He pulled her toward the opening, knocked some more of the glass out with his elbow, then shoved her through.

A jagged edge cut into her leg, but she blocked the pain and leaped to freedom. Colin barreled out the window a few seconds behind her. Dragging in deep gulps of fresh air in between coughs, Emma staggered a safe distance from the blaze.

With Colin next to her, she silently watched as her family cabin burned, flames shooting up into the sky. She took the shirt she'd used to cover her face and pressed it into the bleeding gash on her leg. Numb with fatigue and shock, she was beyond pain as she continued to see a part of her childhood destroyed.

Colin hurried to his SUV and retrieved his cell phone from the front. He called the fire department then J.T.'s office. Listening to him explain what had happened to one of the deputies, Emma knew the cabin would be gone before anyone came.

Colin made his way back to her and wound his arm around her. "Okay?"

"It's gone now…any evidence." Defeat made her drop her head and turn toward Colin.

He embraced her. "Help's on the way."

The wail of the sirens penetrated her hopelessness. Drawing on his comfort, she heard the steady beat of his heart and tried to bolster her demoralized spirit.

A thought flashed into her mind. She raised her head and scanned the area. "What if the person who set the fire is still here watching us?"

Colin looked around while the fire truck and deputy sheriff's car came down the road. He drew her closer, his body almost surrounding hers. "The cavalry's here."

Emma stared at the cabin, now almost completely gone. "For once, too late."

The deputy sheriff walked away from Emma and Colin after getting their statements. With her arms crossed over her chest, Emma watched the firefighters extinguish the blaze, smoke billowing into the sky, darkening the sun. Turning from the smoldering ruins, she noticed several deputies searching the woods around the cabin. She was sure whoever had set the fire was long gone.

A large oak caught her attention. She remembered climbing it one summer and getting stuck up in one of the top branches. Derek had rescued her. The memory brought tears to her eyes, and she closed them for a few seconds.

Not far from the oak stood a thicket of honeysuckle. The time she and Derek had played hide-and-seek and she'd sought refuge in there came unbidden into her thoughts. Scene after scene played across her mind— Derek reading a book to her, teaching her to catch a baseball, hiding their secret stash when she was seven in the well—

Emma straightened and turned around until she saw the old well behind the cabin. *That's it!*

She raced for the well, hoping she was right, hoping whatever Roy and Manny had been after was hidden in there, that it was still there, safe and intact, not lost to them forever.

"Emma," Colin called out to her.

She kept running, needing to find what had been the reason her brother had been killed.

"Emma." His voice sounded nearer.

She stopped at the well and glanced toward Colin a few feet from her. "If Derek hid anything at the cabin, it's in here. One summer it was our secret hiding place."

Colin leaned over. "Down in the water at the bottom?"

"No." She walked around until she found a chip in a red brick. She counted down two and inched a brick out.

Sticking her hand into the hole, she pulled out a packet, wrapped in plastic for protection. She felt as if she had found a national treasure, priceless and irreplaceable.

With quivering fingers, she tore the plastic away and opened the packet. She read what her brother had written, tears flooding her cheeks as she finally realized who was behind Derek's murder and why.

THIRTEEN

"Emma, what is it?" Colin's concerned voice pierced through the pain of betrayal.

"Brandon McDonel had Derek killed. Read for yourself." Her hands shaking, she thrust the packet at Colin while her tears slipped down her face.

Colin read the paper, then looked up at her. "We can't be sure. This is your brother's account of a hit-and-run accident that happened their senior year in college. Brandon was driving and they both had been drinking. The man was killed and the case never solved. That doesn't mean he had Derek murdered."

"You see where Derek was reassessing his life, having second thoughts about remaining quiet, concerned with the lengths Brandon would go to. Maybe he was thinking of coming forward."

"But he would be in trouble, too, even though he wasn't the driver. He witnessed a crime and helped cover it up." Colin massaged the back of his neck, doubt on his face. "I just don't know if that would be reason enough to send hired killers after your brother."

"Brandon's a respected banker in New York, moving up rapidly at his bank. He was recently made vice president, with talk of him moving into the presidency when the present one retired in two years. He had every reason to make sure Derek didn't reveal what happened in college. He had a lot more to lose than Derek. He was the driver." Emma snapped her fingers. "That must be the hit-and-run that Derek had a clipping of in his apartment."

"But why now, after all these years? I don't even know if anything could be done with the statute of limitations. We'd need to ask J.T."

Emma stared off into the woods, remembering her flight through them with Roy and Manny chasing her. "I don't know. I *do* know that when Brandon and I started dating, Derek wasn't happy. That confused me because I always thought of them as good friends, even though they didn't see each other much after college. They roomed together for four years and were very close. That's how I knew Brandon—through my brother."

She shook her head. "Right after Derek came to New York, Brandon backed off and we stopped dating. All of a sudden Brandon had decided he wasn't ready for marriage. I didn't do anything because I wasn't ready, either." Emma tilted her head to the side. "Do you think Derek and Brandon had a confrontation over me?" The very thought that she might be part of the reason her brother had been murdered disturbed her more than the recent attempt on her life.

She pivoted away from Colin, another thought inundating her. She remembered discussing Brandon's proposal with Derek right before he suddenly came to New York. She had been torn between wanting to accept Brandon and not because she was tired of always being alone. She and Brandon had gotten along well, enjoyed a lot of the same things. Although Brandon had come from a poor family, he had become very successful. She had been using her brother as a sounding board. Was that phone call to Derek what had started everything?

Later, when she had said something to her brother about Brandon backing off, Derek had consoled her, saying Brandon wasn't good enough for her. He had pointed out his poor background from the South Side of Chicago. He had— She dropped her head into her hands, finally recalling what had been nagging her all along.

"Emma?" Colin came around to stand in front of her, compelling her to look him in the eye. "We'll give this to J.T. and let him sort it out. We don't know anything for sure. It could still be someone else."

"It's Brandon. I remember why I always felt I had known Roy from somewhere. I met him once years ago in Chicago while with Brandon and Derek. Roy is from Brandon's old neighborhood and they had been childhood friends. I don't usually forget a face, but sometimes it takes me a while to recall where I've seen someone and who he is."

Colin stiffened, his hands knotting into fists. "That's different. We need to let J.T. know right away. They can pick him up and hopefully get to the bottom of this. And with the connection between Roy and Brandon, maybe Roy will decide it's in his best interest to turn state's evidence."

Hugging her arms to her, Emma shuddered. She recalled the day before when Brandon had embraced her, pressing her close to him as though they were still dating.

"Let's get out of here. J.T. will be back from Chicago by now."

* * *

"Roy won't talk," J.T. said when he entered his office with Emma and Colin. "But Manny is."

Emma stopped dead in her tracks. "He is? That's great! What's he saying?"

J.T. indicated the two straight-back chairs in front of his desk and took his own behind it. "He confirmed that Brandon McDonel hired them to kill Derek and to get all the information on the hit-and-run accident. Brandon knew that your brother had written out an accounting of the accident because Derek was threatening to reveal what happened all those years ago. Brandon was tired of your brother's blackmailing."

Emma wilted in the chair. "Blackmailing? Derek?"

"Apparently he'd told Brandon if he didn't stop seeing you he would. He didn't care any longer how his involvement keeping the accident quiet all those years ago looked to the world. Then a month ago, your brother called Brandon up and needed some financial information concerning his partner. He had an account at Brandon's bank. Brandon gave Derek the information he wanted, but he didn't think that would be the end of it, so he had Roy and Manny keep tabs on your brother."

Derek hadn't been innocent in this whole affair, but he hadn't deserved to die. Emma's fingernails dug into her palms. "What about Brandon? Is he here yet?"

"He should be here any minute. Madison and one of my deputies are transporting him from Chicago."

"You'll let us know what he says." Colin stood, deep circles beneath his eyes.

Colin hadn't gotten any more sleep than she had from the looks of him. Every time she had closed her eyes, she had relived the cabin fire and the discovery of her brother's account of the hit-and-run. A thought came to mind. Why had Brandon gone to such extremes? "J.T., you might want to investigate this hit-and-run. I realize the accident would have hurt Brandon at the bank, but since the statute of limitations had run out, why did he have my brother killed over the threat of exposure? Was there something else going on?"

"Good point. We'll look into it. It'll help in building our case against Brandon McDonel."

"We have the newspaper clipping about the accident that we retrieved from Derek's apartment. We'll get the whole folder to you. Maybe it can help you now that we know there's a connection."

"I appreciate it, Emma. I know none of this is easy for you, but at least you're safe now."

Safe. Yes, and now she had to rebuild her life. Emma rose. "I'll be here another day or so then I'll be returning to New York. When you need me, I'll be back." She reached across J.T.'s desk and shook his hand. "Thank you."

Emma followed Colin to the door. Out in the hallway she paused, leaning back against the wall. Lack of sleep was catching up with her. There was so much she needed to do, and yet she couldn't seem to put two coherent thoughts together. She wanted to sleep the day away but was afraid she couldn't.

"Emma, you can stay as long as you need."

She offered Colin a smile. "I know. Grace already told me this morning. But I have to straighten out my life. So much has changed and yet somehow it hasn't. I still have a business in New York and jobs that are lined up, people depending on me. I have to see to Derek's estate. I—" She came to a halt, the list in her mind seemingly endless and suddenly monumental.

Colin took in her tired expression, a dull glint in her eyes, a pale cast to her features. More than anything he wanted to hug her and never let her go. But he wouldn't do that. He couldn't add to the dilemmas she faced. He wanted to make a life with her. But she needed to discover just who she was and where the Lord fit into her new life. He loved her and he had to let her go. He'd come to that decision late last night while trying to sleep.

He held out his hand. "Let's go—to Grace's." He'd almost said home. For some reason, with her it felt so right.

She fit hers within his and began walking toward the entrance to the sheriff's office, her pace slow. Outside the sun shone bright, the sky a cloudless blue. A light breeze blew from the west, gently stirring the warm air imbued with the scents of spring.

A squad car pulling into the parking lot in front marred the beautiful day. Madison exited and opened the back door to allow Brandon to climb out, his hands cuffed. Colin started to step in Emma's line of vision, but her gasp alerted him to the fact she'd seen Brandon.

For a few seconds she stared at her brother's murderer, frozen as though a sudden snowstorm had descended. Then suddenly she surged forward, intercepting Brandon at the door into the sheriff's office. He looked right at her, his eyes narrowed, his mouth pinched into a scowl.

Emma opened her mouth to say something, stopped for a few seconds, then muttered, "Not worth it," before stepping to the side to let the trio enter the building.

She came back to him, passed in front and headed for his SUV without a backward glance at Brandon. The man paused in the doorway into the sheriff's office, his gaze glued to Emma. Puzzlement marked his features.

When Colin slipped behind the steering wheel, he tossed a look toward Emma. "What changed your mind?"

"I had all the intention of telling Brandon McDonel exactly what I thought of him. For a moment I was so angry. But suddenly I remembered some lines from a psalm I read last night when I was trying to sleep and couldn't. 'The Lord is gracious and full of compassion; slow to anger and of great mercy.' The words comforted me last night and they have again today. I'm not at the place where I can forgive Brandon for what he did, but hopefully I can one day, because I don't like what anger does to me."

Hearing her talk about God heartened Colin. Her growing faith was one good thing that had come out of all that had happened—that and his love for Emma. He hadn't thought himself capable of loving again, but he did.

"You're really leaving us," Amber said, plopping down on the bed while Emma finished folding her last garment and placed it in her bag.

"I need to get back to New York. I've stayed—" Emma swallowed her words, not able to say she'd stayed long enough, because she didn't feel that way.

"Why? What's there in New York?"

Good question, Emma thought, and closed her suitcase. She sat down next to the teenager. "My job, for one."

"Don't you mostly fly to shoots?"

"Sometimes."

"But I thought you and Dad were getting along so well."

"We were. Are. I consider him a good friend. After all, he saved my life on a number of occasions."

"I wish you would stay."

How could she explain to Amber her confusion and insecurity? She wasn't the same woman who had left New York a few weeks before. How could she start a new life until she knew who she really was? Where did her faith enter into her lifestyle? Even her relationship with her father was changing. Nothing was the same, especially her ability to distance herself from others, which she had been so good at before coming to Crystal Springs. She'd fallen in love with Colin, but under such extraordinary circumstances, were her feelings true love? She never wanted to hurt him or his family. If she didn't figure that out, then she could.

Colin coughed. Emma looked toward the doorway. He lounged against the jamb, his arms and legs crossed in a casual stance. But the expression on his face held a troubled countenance. He masked it quickly but not quickly enough. Emma had seen his concern.

Amber hugged her, then murmured something about getting Tiffany and hurried from the room. Emma rose slowly from the bed, her eyes connected to Colin's. The warmth that invaded his features permeated her, making her wonder how in the world she could walk away from him.

"All packed?" he asked, pushing himself away from the doorjamb and covering the space between them, everything casual about him now from the way he walked to his tone of voice and his expression.

She nodded, suddenly not able to form any words. His looks, his nearness stole her breath. Finally she was able to ask, "Have you heard any more from J.T.?"

"Brandon isn't talking, but Roy has decided to, so the case is looking good. Madison discovered another reason, beyond hurting Brandon's reputation, why Brandon may have hired Roy and Manny to kill Derek. With further investigation it's looking like Brandon didn't accidentally hit that man. He may have done it on purpose, which would make it murder. There's no statute of limitations on murder."

"On purpose? Why?" she asked. She wanted to get even closer to Colin but held herself back. It wouldn't change the fact that she needed to leave. In fact, it would only complicate the situation. Besides, Colin had never asked her to stay with him.

"I don't think your brother realized that Brandon had known the person he hit with his car that night. He had just had a fight with that person the day before over something to do with the old neighborhood. The police in Chicago are reopening the hit-and-run case now that they know of the connection."

"You think you know someone and you really don't. First, my brother and now Brandon." She blew a breath of air out through pursed lips. "My record isn't looking too good."

Colin stepped toward her and touched her arm. "How your brother was with you was true. He wasn't faking his love and caring."

"But who can say that with Brandon? He is like a Dr. Jekyll and Mr. Hyde."

"There are people in the world who sadly are. Often they get by fooling everyone around them. But usually it catches up with them. Like Brandon. He'll pay for his crimes."

"So it's finally over. Really."

"Yup. You have nothing to worry about. You'll be safe and can put your life back together."

Without you, she thought, a throbbing ache causing her heart to pulsate slowly. "Yes. According to my assistant, everything was put on hold because my clients wanted me to do the photo shoots, not someone else."

A half smile curved his mouth. "It's nice being in demand."

And so busy I might not have time to miss you. She hoped so, because already she dreaded the thought of not seeing him every day. "I have a lot of work piled up, that's for sure."

Colin bent down and grabbed the handle of the piece of luggage. "I've got a present for you."

As he started for the hallway, Emma asked, "What?"

He peered over his shoulder. "It's a surprise. You'll have to wait."

She hurried after him, following him to the foyer where Tiffany, Amber and Grace were lined up waiting for her. On the table was a gold-and-white-wrapped gift with a huge bow. Colin picked it up and gave it to her.

"You shouldn't have," she said, tearing into the present. She'd always loved doing that at Christmas and her birthday. She didn't want gift bags, but presents wrapped with paper. When she glimpsed the Bible with her name engraved on the front, tears sprang to her eyes. "Oh, I love it."

"I thought you needed one of your own."

She tucked it against her heart. "Thank you all—for everything."

She turned to Tiffany first, giving her a hug and kiss. Next came Amber then Grace. Finally she stood in front of Colin. She looked down at the floor for a moment, her mind blank. How did you tell someone who had saved your life three times goodbye? How did you tell someone you *loved* goodbye? Words didn't express what she felt—the confusion, the heartache, the fear of what lay ahead without Colin. He'd given her the tools to piece her life back together. With God's guidance, she could figure out who she was and where she really belonged.

Colin tilted up her chin and searched her face. "We'll miss you." He brushed his lips across hers, fleetingly, then backed away.

She wanted to capture him and hold on to him. She wanted a kiss that branded her his. She wanted…to stay? How could she know for sure that was what was best even if he had asked her to—which he hadn't? No, she was doing the right thing, returning to New York and her old life.

The ringing of the doorbell told her it was time to leave. That would be her father, and staying any longer would only prolong the hurt. Taking her bag, she strode to the door and opened it, greeting her father with a smile.

He said a few words to Grace and Colin, adding his thanks, then relieved her of her piece of luggage. She walked beside him to the limousine waiting in the driveway.

"I thought about driving myself, but this will give us some time to get reacquainted before you have to catch your flight. Your car will be waiting for you in New York. I'm glad you didn't drive back by yourself."

Emma slid into the backseat, refusing to look toward Grace's house. Her throat closed, she poured herself a glass of ice water and downed half of it.

As the limousine pulled away, her father asked, "Are you sure you want to leave?"

Another deep gulp of her cold water and she thought she could answer her father without faltering. "Yes, it's for the best. I can't picture myself living in a small town."

"Sugar, it's been six months. Don't you think it's about time you went and saw her?" Grace asked, sitting next to Colin at her kitchen table.

Colin took a sip of his coffee. He'd asked himself that very question ever since Emma had left last May—an eternity ago. He knew how she was doing because she and Amber e-mailed each other and kept in touch on a weekly basis. But he hadn't seen her—unless he counted the pictures he'd seen in the newspaper and magazines—or talked to her in six months. A clean break, he'd told himself when she'd left. She'd needed to sort out her life without him complicating it, and he'd needed to start the healing process all over again. His heart still bled, though, and he dreamed of her every night. He wasn't being very successful in that department.

"Colin! Did you hear me?"

His aunt's voice urged him to answer her question when he had no answer. "Yes. I was thinking."

"Duh. You do that a lot lately. At least, call her. The holidays are coming up. Thanksgiving is next week."

"Amber said she was spending it with her father."

"She'll be in Chicago? That's great. That's not far away." Grace drank from her patriotic mug. "Okay, I've pussyfooted around this long enough. Do you love her?"

With all my heart, he thought, not wanting to say it out loud for fear any inroads on healing would be undone.

"Do you?"

His aunt wouldn't give up. That was what he liked about her—and disliked at times. "Yes."

"Then go see her. Tell her how you feel. Knowing you, you didn't say anything to her about how you felt."

"How could I? That wouldn't have been right. She needed to grieve for her brother. For that matter, she needed to grieve over losing a friend."

Grace snorted. "McDonel was no friend."

"Yeah, but she didn't know that. They dated. Might have gotten married."

"If her brother hadn't stepped in."

"She wasn't ready to hear my declaration of love."

"You might be right, but she'll be now. Amber says she's doing great. She's in such demand."

"That's another reason. How can I ask her to marry me and give up all that because I won't move my family to New York?"

"She's a photographer. She can be based anywhere. Her reputation is established. People come to her, not the other way around." Grace pushed her chair back and rose. She went to the coffeepot and refilled her mug. "I've never known you to avoid a situation. What are you afraid of?"

"Emma saying no. When Mary Ann died, I thought

a part of me had died with her. Now I discover I'm very much alive and hurting all over again. If she said no, my hope that I've harbored this past six months will die."

"Colin Fitzpatrick! I can't believe what I'm hearing. You've always gone after what you've wanted. If Emma is what you want, then you should be on the next plane out of here. I'll take care of the girls."

Colin stared at the coffee in the bottom of his cup, his heart pounding against his chest as though it were going to escape.

Was six months long enough?

There was only one way to find out.

Staring out her apartment window, Emma caught a glimpse of Central Park as the sun set, a brilliant yellow-orange streaking through the darkening sky. The color reminded her of the flames that had destroyed the cabin at Crystal Springs. That thought brought her to the call she had received from the district attorney in charge of prosecuting Brandon for her brother's murder.

She would have to go back to Crystal Springs after the new year and face everything again. The prospect scared her, and yet she was ready to put that part of her life behind her. She'd mourned Derek's loss for the past six months and would for the rest of her life. Along the line, she had come to terms with the picture she had of her brother and the one he'd presented to the rest of the world. Studying the Bible in detail had helped her to forgive.

Now what did she do? Keep working and going through the motions of living? Or do something radical like leave New York and return to Crystal Springs, not for the trial, but to live? Since she had returned to the city, none of the previous joy of living in New York satisfied her. She wanted something different. She was different. She wanted Colin. She wanted a loving family—the kind in storybooks where everyone lived happily ever after.

The phone ringing startled her. She hurried to answer it, pleased to hear from her father.

"I'll pick you up at the airport next Tuesday. I'm glad you're coming for Thanksgiving. I haven't had a traditional Thanksgiving dinner in years."

Her father's deep, gravelly voice filled her with renewed hope that their relationship was moving in a good direction. It hadn't been easy. He still liked to dictate, but now he was willing to compromise and listen to her. "I'm looking forward to seeing you again. Your visit last month wasn't long enough."

"You can always stay longer than five days. You could move here."

For the first time she said, "Maybe."

"Maybe? Did I hear you correctly?"

"Dad, I'm not ruling out anything at the moment. We'll talk more when I get there."

"Are you going to drive down to Crystal Springs while you're here?"

Emma released a long sigh. A good question. She loved Colin, but she really wasn't sure how he felt. Six months before, too much had been up in the air to push forward in a relationship. Now though, she had a grasp on who she was and what she wanted.

"Emma?"

"Sorry, Dad, I'm debating with myself on that one."

"He's a good man, Emma. You could do a lot worse."

She laughed. "That's quite an endorsement coming from you."

"What can I say? He saved your life in more ways than one."

"Yes, he did," she murmured, thinking of her growing faith in Jesus and the peace it brought her, a peace she'd never felt before.

The doorbell chimed. "Dad, I've got to go. My dinner is here."

His chuckles floated to her. "Still haven't learned to cook."

She smiled at her father's comment as she rushed toward the foyer. She was cooking more, but she would probably never be like Grace. Swinging the door open, she gasped. Next to the pizza delivery guy stood Colin with a huge grin on his handsome face.

He paid the young man, took the pizza box and came into her apartment while all she could do was stare at him. Her mind swirled, but no thought would come to the foreground. She stepped back as she closed the door and looked toward Colin.

"It's good to see you again, Emma. This is a nice place."

She planted her hand on the table in the foyer to keep herself from collapsing to the marble floor. He looked every bit as wonderful as she remembered. Every part of her screamed to throw herself into his arms, but she remained where she was, standing on trembling legs.

"Do you want to eat before we talk?" He held up the pizza box.

She blinked, shaking her head slightly. "I don't think

it would stay down." Her stomach flip-flopped at that very moment to prove her point.

"Good." He tossed the box on the table and held out his hand for her.

She took it, the warmth of his touch searing his presence in her mind. This wasn't one of her dreams. He tugged her forward into her living room, which sprawled before the large floor-to-ceiling windows across one wall. Darkness fell behind the glass panes, lights from the city glittering in the blackness.

He pulled her down on the white couch and settled her next to him. "I've been rehearsing my speech the whole way here and I've forgotten every word I was going to say—a man used to memorizing pages of a sermon. Guess it's the company I'm keeping."

She slanted a look at him. "Thanks, I think." The grin that split her face had to be silly if it reflected the giddiness she felt.

"So I'll get right to the point. I love you, Emma St. James. I've left you alone long enough."

"Why did you?"

"You needed time to grieve, to decide what you wanted. Me hanging around would have complicated that for you."

"Then what I felt developing between us in Crystal Springs wasn't a figment of my imagination?"

He slowly shook his head, a gleam in his eyes. "Not one bit. You don't know how many times I almost chucked my noble intentions and came to see you."

"I wish you had."

"Do you really?"

She chuckled. "Well, maybe it was for the best you

stayed away. Truthfully, it's only been recently that I've come to the place I want to be."

"Which is?" One of his eyebrows rose.

"Your wife."

His mouth fell open. She leaned forward and kissed him.

"I love you, Colin Fitzpatrick. I knew that when I left Crystal Springs. I just didn't know if I was right for you or if you were right for me."

"And you do now?" He hauled her up against him.

She wound her arms around him. "Oh, yes, most definitely. You showed me my way out of the dark."

"I hope you don't want a long engagement. I've waited long enough."

Her laughter bubbled from her throat and gratified her with such peace. "I'm ready, anytime, anywhere."

EPILOGUE

"Pass the ham, please," Amber said to Emma.

She lifted the large platter and gave it to Amber, who sat on her left. "Dad, are you going to be able to stay a few days this time?"

"I've cleared my calendar. You've got me for the whole Christmas week."

Colin took her hand and held it between their chairs. "You're always welcome in our home, William."

Our home, Emma thought, scanning the dining room where they were gathered for their first Christmas meal as a family. The first one she'd ever really had in her life.

She'd been married exactly three wonderful weeks. In that time she had gained a family, a congregation and a home. Even with the trial coming up the next month, she would have Colin beside her the whole time. She would be able to face anything with him and the Lord on her side.

"Maybe you'd like to come watch me cheer at the basketball game on Thursday night. Our team is first in its division. My boyfriend plays forward." Tiffany brought her hand up, waving it with fingers splayed. "Did I show you the bracelet Brent gave me for Christmas?"

Colin choked on the water he was drinking. Emma patted him on the back while Amber said, "About fifty times."

"You're just jealous," Tiffany fired back.

"Girls." Grace rose and went into her kitchen. When she came back out, she said, "Emma, you forgot to put your green bean casserole on the table."

She sank lower in her chair. "No, I didn't. I took a taste of it and decided we had enough food already."

Colin laughed. "Good thing Grace gave you those cooking lessons for Christmas."

The good-natured ribbing that commenced only strengthened Emma's love for each one at the table. This was what family was all about. The dark veil over her life had been lifted when she met Colin and gave herself to the Lord.

* * * * *

Look for Margaret Daley's next book,
VANISHED,
coming only from Love Inspired Suspense,
in May, 2007.
Once again, J. T. Logan and Madison Spencer
are working together…this time to find
J.T.'s kidnapped little girl!

Dear Reader,

This story was a very emotional one to write. What would happen if something precious such as my eyesight was taken away from me? So often we take our eyesight for granted. That is one of the premises of this book. I have worked with students who are visually impaired and seen their perseverance and determination to make their lives as normal as possible. My mother-in-law, who loves to read, has been dealing with low vision because of a disease. It changed her life. She has had to adjust to doing everyday things differently. Writing this book made me take a good hard look at taking for granted something such as my eyesight. This story was a journey for me as well as Emma, who had to learn to put her trust in God to see her through her ordeal.

I love hearing from readers. You can contact me at P.O. Box 2074, Tulsa, OK 74101, or visit my Web site at www.margaretdaley.com. Sign my guest book for a chance to win a free autographed book and sign up for my quarterly newsletter.

Best wishes,

Margaret Daley

QUESTIONS FOR DISCUSSION

1) How would you deal with losing your eyesight suddenly? How would that impact your life?

2) Have you lost a loved one? How did you cope? Did your faith help you through the loss?

3) Colin felt responsible for Emma's accident. Have you ever felt responsible for hurting another? How did you handle it?

4) Who did you think was behind Emma's brother's murder? Why?

5) Emma had to put her trust in the Lord to make it through an ordeal. Has that happened to you? How have you dealt with it?

6) Trust is so important in a relationship and is a theme in *So Dark the Night*. Can you think of a Bible verse that would help Emma learn to put her trust in the Lord and Colin?

7) Emma's parents were divorced and put Emma in the middle of their fighting. If you were put in the middle of a conflict between two people you loved, what could you do to make the situation better?

8) Who was your favorite character? Why?

9) Colin had to harm a person in order to protect himself and Emma. How far would you go to protect someone you loved?

10) Emma had to learn to negotiate a strange house without her eyesight. What have you learned lately that is totally alien to you?

REQUEST YOUR FREE BOOKS!

2 FREE INSPIRATIONAL NOVELS
PLUS 2
FREE
MYSTERY GIFTS

Love Inspired

YES! Please send me 2 FREE Love Inspired® novels and my 2 FREE mystery gifts. After receiving them, if I don't wish to receive any more books, I can return the shipping statement marked "cancel." If I don't cancel, I will receive 4 brand-new novels every month and be billed just $3.99 per book in the U.S., or $4.74 per book in Canada, plus 25¢ shipping and handling per book and applicable taxes, if any*. That's a savings of 20% off the cover price! I understand that accepting the 2 free books and gifts places me under no obligation to buy anything. I can always return a shipment and cancel at any time. Even if I never buy another book from Steeple Hill, the two free books and gifts are mine to keep forever.

113 IDN EF26   313 IDN EF27

Name	(PLEASE PRINT)	
Address		Apt. #
City	State/Prov.	Zip/Postal Code

Signature (if under 18, a parent or guardian must sign)

Order online at www.LoveInspiredBooks.com

Or mail to Steeple Hill Reader Service™:

IN U.S.A.: P.O. Box 1867, Buffalo, NY 14240-1867
IN CANADA: P.O. Box 609, Fort Erie, Ontario L2A 5X3

Not valid to current Love Inspired subscribers.

Want to try two free books from another series?
Call 1-800-873-8635 or visit www.morefreebooks.com

* Terms and prices subject to change without notice. NY residents add applicable sales tax. Canadian residents will be charged applicable provincial taxes and GST. This offer is limited to one order per household. All orders subject to approval. Credit or debit balances in a customer's account(s) may be offset by any other outstanding balance owed by or to the customer. Please allow 4 to 6 weeks for delivery.

Your Privacy: Steeple Hill is committed to protecting your privacy. Our Privacy Policy is available online at www.eHarlequin.com or upon request from the Reader Service. From time to time we make our lists of customers available to reputable firms who may have a product or service of interest to you. If you would prefer we not share your name and address, please check here. ☐

LIREG07

Love Inspired SUSPENSE

TITLES AVAILABLE NEXT MONTH

Don't miss these four stories in April

DANGEROUS SEASON by Lyn Cote
Harbor Intrigue

Sheriff Keir Harding hoped to put his troubled past behind him—until an arsonist threatened his community. Keir enlisted the aid of Audra Blair, but could he ever forgive himself if she paid the ultimate price for getting involved?

THE SOUND OF SECRETS by Irene Brand
The Secrets of Stoneley

The night she found her mother murdered, Nerissa Blanchard was grateful for the quiet strength of Officer Drew Lancaster. But the strange happenings that followed had her wondering if she was losing her mind—or if someone wanted to silence her forever.

NOWHERE TO HIDE by Debby Giusti

Lydia Sloan's husband's killer wanted her son to be his next victim. Fearing for their safety, she fled. She soon realized security guard Matt Lawson was the only one she could trust with her secret and her child's life.

CAUGHT IN THE MIDDLE by Gayle Roper

Newspaper reporter Merry Kramer was horrified to find a dead body in her car. Surrounded by suspects, she'd have to use all her investigative skills to keep from becoming front-page news as the killer's next victim.

LISCNM0307